Running
on the
Cracks

Running
on the
Cracks

Julia Donaldson

HENRY HOLT AND COMPANY

NEW YORK

Henry Holt and Company, LLC
Publishers since 1866
175 Fifth Avenue
New York, New York 10010
www.HenryHoltKids.com

First published in the United States in 2009 by Henry Holt and Company, LLC.
Originally published in the United Kingdom in 2009 by Egmont UK Ltd.

Library of Congress Cataloging-in-Publication Data
Donaldson, Julia.
Running on the cracks / Julia Donaldson.—1st American ed.
p.   cm.
Summary: After her parents are killed in an accident, English teenager
Leonora Watts-Chan runs away to Glasgow, Scotland, to find her Chinese
grandparents.
ISBN 978-0-8050-9054-3
[1. Runaways— Fiction. 2. Orphans—Fiction. 3. Sexual abuse victims—Fiction.
4. Chinese—Scotland—Fiction. 5. Racially mixed people—
Fiction. 6. Glasgow (Scotland)—Fiction. 7. Scotland—Fiction.] I. Title.
PZ7.D71499Ru 2009   [Fic]—dc22   2008050278

First American Edition—2009 / Designed by Véronique Lefèvre Sweet
Printed in the United States of America.

10 9 8 7 6 5 4 3 2 1

To my sons, Ally and Jerry,
and in memory of Hamish

LEO
Station Loo

This is the bit I've planned. I know what I've got to do, but it would help if my hands would stop shaking.

It would help if there was more space too. I should have gone into the disabled loo instead of the ladies. The cubicle is tiny; the gap under the door feels huge. What if anyone peers under it? Instead of seeing two feet plonked apart facing forward, they'll see a bulky school bag and various clothes going in and out of it.

First, off comes the brand-new, snooty blazer with the high school crest on it. Poor blazer—it'll never enter the high school now.

A door swings. Footsteps, coming toward me. Another door bangs in my ear. Someone is in the loo next to mine. I freeze with my tie half unknotted.

Don't be so paranoid! No one's looking for me yet.

I unbutton the white shirt and slip out of the black skirt.

An echoey announcement wafts through the air. It's for the Exeter train, not mine, but there's not much time left.

I rummage in the school bag. Beneath the empty files

and folders and the unused gym kit is my precious sketch-book. That's not what I'm looking for, though it's good to feel its familiar battered corners.

Here it is, the secret carrier bag. And inside it, the jumble-sale clothes.

I still think that jumble sale was a brainwave. A total disguise, and such a cheap one—only £3.50 altogether for the beige hooded anorak, the white T-shirt and red sweater, the definitely nondesigner jeans and trainers (how Caitlin and Flo would slag me off if they saw them!), and the pair of sunglasses.

Actually, I'm not so sure about the sunglasses anymore. Maybe they'll just draw attention to me. After all, the clothes aren't summery. In fact, they're too hot for this warm September day, but then Glasgow is bound to be colder than Bristol, and it'll be winter all too soon.

Now for the cleverest trick of all. Folded up inside the carrier bag is a flimsy nylon hold-all—another jumble-sale bargain. It cost all of 40p and is big enough to contain my school bag and all its contents. Now I won't have to leave the school bag in the station or risk having it spotted and identified on the train.

The hold-all even has a zip pocket for my purse. No need to check the contents of the purse, really, but I do: £39.60 and a ticket.

The wrong ticket.

That's all right, though; it's all part of the plan. Instead of a ticket to Glasgow, I've bought a standard day single to Paddington. The ticket will be as unused as the school uniform, and it cost a lot more than the jumble-sale clothes, but it was worth it. Along with my note, it should put them off the scent for a while. "I'm going to see the Dali exhibition at the Tate Britain," I told the ticket clerk. He'll remember me now. That's the plan anyway.

The £39.60 is just enough to pay for my ticket on the Glasgow train if I have to, but I do hope I won't. I'm planning some more sneaky visits to the loo, timed to coincide with any ticket inspections.

I remember Mum's scorn for fare-dodgers. "Sorry, Mum, but this is different," I tell her. I don't really believe in heaven, but I still find myself talking to her—and to Dad too.

The transformation is complete, and the ladies is all mine again. Furtively—no, casually; I mustn't look furtive—I emerge and look at myself in the mirror.

The clothes and hold-all are nondescript, which is the effect I wanted. My face is unfortunately not nondescript at all. I look Chinese, like Dad, instead of English like Mum. (For some reason, thinking about Mum and Dad isn't hurting so much as usual. I suppose the excitement and nerves are covering up the hurt.) If my hair had been long, I could maybe have cut it, but it's short, black, and shiny. Hood up? Hood down? Sunglasses on? Off?

No time for dithering, as a crescendo of train wheels

and a floating announcement remind me: "The nine forty-five for Glasgow Central is now arriving at platform one. Calling at Cheltenham Spa, Birmingham New Street, Preston, Carlisle, and Motherwell. Platform one for the nine forty-five to Glasgow Central."

Suddenly I feel sick. It's the thought of all those stops and starts. It's going to be a long journey, and I don't know what's at the other end.

FINLAY
Through the Letter Box

"Who's walked off with those bloody *Telegraph* supplements?" Rab was in his normal mood, shouting at any paperboy within earshot and filling the already thick air of the depot with yet more cigarette smoke.

"I saw you put that pile of *Herald*s on top of them," said Finlay.

Rab shot him an ungrateful glance. "What's that black muck on your fingernails?" he asked.

"Nail varnish," said Finlay with a faint sigh that was intended to be withering.

Rab gave his nearest to a chuckle. "What do they call that shade, then? Black Death?"

Actually, it *was* called that, but Finlay wasn't going to tell Rab. The nail varnish had been a bargain at the Barras market; so had the spiky bracelet. They'd have been more than twice the price in Inferno.

Finlay scooped up his bundle of papers. BODY FOUND BY BIN MAN was the headline on the *Morning Post* at the top of the pile. As he rammed the papers into the luminous yellow bag with the strap designed to cripple young shoulders, he had a vision of himself as a modern-day Oliver Twist. Rab was Fagin, of course—exploiting his troop of innocent defenseless paperboys, stunting them, insulting them, poisoning the air they breathed.

"If you get any of that Black Death on the papers, you'll be the next body in the bin!" Rab yelled after him.

"You've just dropped ash on the *Scotsman*," Finlay couldn't resist calling over his shoulder. It was the sort of remark that would get him into trouble at school or at home—"answering back," as it was unfairly called by his teachers and parents, who considered they were the only ones entitled to make personal remarks, but old Rab wasn't going to hand out a Notification of Misconduct form or order him to tidy his room and couldn't afford to sack him. Finlay had only been doing the paper round for three weeks, but he felt he had the measure of Rab: His bark was worse than his bite.

Who were the sadists who designed and positioned letter boxes? There were the ones at the very bottom of the door, so you had to kneel in a puddle to push the paper in, the ones that always tore the paper (maybe they had a cunningly concealed serrated edge), and the ones that resisted newspapers altogether, preferring to snap hands off.

The garden gates were almost as bad. Some didn't want to open, and some didn't want to close—but if you left them open, you could be sure that some Neighborhood Watch busybody would spot you and complain.

Finlay was relieved when he reached the block of flats on the corner of Struan Drive. This was the easiest building—no gates, no paths blocked by wheely bins or burst bin-liners. It only took about two minutes to deliver ten papers to the flats.

He tramped up the stairs, enjoying their echo. His feet beat out the heavy rhythm of "Stone Sacrifice" from Breakneck's new album. When he reached the second floor, the strap across his shoulder transformed itself into a guitar strap and he played the solo in his head as he fumbled for the *Morning Post*. Here it was: "McNally, 2/1" scrawled across the top above the BODY FOUND BY BIN MAN headline.

But there were already two papers poking out of 2/1's letter box. Today was Tuesday. He dimly remembered now that the weekend paper had still been there yesterday.

Maybe McNally 2/1, whoever he or she was, had gone away on holiday and forgotten to cancel the papers.

Or maybe they were ill. Maybe they'd had a stroke and were lying on the carpet, trying to claw themselves toward the phone.

Maybe they were dead.

Finlay pushed today's *Morning Post* into the letter box. Instead of thudding down to the floor, it stuck beside the two others; this must be one of those doors with a wire cage inside it to catch the post. He squatted, pushed the metal flap up a bit, and peered inside. There was a light on.

That didn't mean anything. Maybe they'd left it on to fool would-be burglars.

Was there a smell coming from the flat, or was he just imagining it? A ripe, meaty kind of smell—not mouthwateringly meaty, though; nothing like bacon or burgers. Could it be the smell of a fresh human corpse?

What was the time? Finlay glanced at his wrist before remembering that he'd discarded his embarrassing watch in favor of the new spiky bracelet. But it must be about twenty to nine. He ought to get a move on. There were five more floors in the flats and then the whole of Endred Close to do. He was going to be late for school again as it was.

But in his mind he could see the headline, BODY FOUND BY PAPERBOY.

Finlay wasn't sure if he wanted to find a body or not, but if there was a body to be found, he didn't want someone else to find it. He didn't want to be in the small print: "Neighbors and even the regular paperboy had failed to spot telltale signs."

He put down his paper bag and tapped at the door. Silence. He tapped again, louder. Silence. Or was there something? A faint thud? He pushed the letter box again and peered in.

Two green eyes in a tabby face stared up at him. The cat opened its mouth in a silent meow.

"Whit d'ye think ye're doing?"

Finlay spun round. A grim-looking woman in a fleecy dressing gown was standing in the doorway of flat 2/2.

"I was just a wee bit worried about Mr. . . . Mrs. . . . McNally," he spluttered.

"*Miss* McNally," said Dressing Gown, eyeing him up and down. She obviously thought he was up to no good.

"She's not been collecting her papers. Do you think she's all right?"

Dressing Gown's scowl softened slightly.

"She'll just be having one of her downers, that's all. This time next week she'll be dancing the Dashing White Sergeant. All night long, knowing her."

"I see," said Finlay, though he didn't really. "Is her cat all right?"

"Oh, aye, right as rain. She'll neglect herself but no' the moggie. She spends all her benefit on cat food, that one does."

Of course—that ripe meaty smell, fresh but mildly revolting, had been the smell of cat food. Finlay should have recognized it, considering the number of times Mum had made him feed Mungo even though she knew it made him want to puke.

Dressing Gown wasn't volunteering any more, but she

stayed in her doorway; under her scrutiny there wasn't anything Finlay could do other than shoulder his bag and clatter on up the echoey stairs. He couldn't get back into the rhythm of "Stone Sacrifice," and he felt foolish to have been carried away by fantasy. Now he would definitely be late for school. He would miss registration yet again, and that almost certainly meant another Notification of Misconduct form to be taken home and signed by Mum or Dad. Another N of M form meant no pocket money next week. And that meant the electric guitar was one week further away. At this rate, he'd never get to be in Ross McGovern's band.

Well, there was nothing he could do about that now. Except, perhaps . . . Finlay's thoughts turned from corpses to forgery.

LEO ▨ ▨ ▨
Midnight Oil

It's three in the morning, and I'm trying to keep my eyes open. I'm in an all-night café. It's not like the one in "The Streets of London" that's full of down-and-outs carrying their home in two carrier bags. Unless you count me, that is. I suppose *I'm* a down-and-out, and I'm carrying my home in one nylon hold-all (which is, in fact, holding not a lot).

The café is called Midnight Oil, and there are old-fashioned oil lamps on all the tables. There's a blue bath full of plants and a green one full of goldfish. The walls are purple and covered in mirrors, which I notice are for sale, but I don't think I'll spend my remaining thirty-four pounds on one of them.

The menu has all sorts of coffee and hot chocolate, with whipped cream, hazelnut, cinnamon, tiramisu—you name it. I've been sticking to tea, which is a bit cheaper (but quite enough—£1.50), and resisting the food.

This wasn't in the plan. I'd been looking for the youth hostel when I stumbled on this place, but this is a cheaper and maybe a less conspicuous way of spending my first night in Glasgow. The staff are quite young—students, I suppose—and the shifts keep changing, so they don't all know how long I've been sitting here.

There are other people sitting by themselves: a man with a mobile phone, a woman with a book of puzzles. I don't think anyone is giving me suspicious looks, but then it would look a bit suspicious if I kept looking 'round for suspicious looks.

Instead, I'm pretending to be immersed in the evening paper, which I now know off by heart. There's nothing in it about me, but I suppose there wouldn't be, yet. It's this morning's papers I'm dreading.

My plan for the day is written in my head:

1. Buy some cheap food
2. Get some sleep (where? a park bench if it's not raining?)

3. Find a library where I can
    a) read today's papers
    b) look up all the Chans in the phone book
4. Start looking for . . .

What shall I call them? Granny and Grandpa? You never taught me the Chinese for those words, did you, Dad? But then you hardly ever talked about them. How I wish, wish, wish I'd asked you more, before it was too late.

Here's what I *do* know about them and about your childhood:

They owned their own restaurant, but I don't even know what it was called. There must be dozens of Chinese restaurants in Glasgow.

They lived in the basement of a tenement house quite near the restaurant, and you were their only child. All I know about the flat is that there was an alcove in the kitchen where you used to sleep. Oh, and that there was a square nearby with a big sycamore tree in it. (I know that because there was a sycamore in our London garden too. Mum always complained that it stole the light, but you liked it; you showed me how you used to pick up the winged seeds and twirl them in the air and pretend they were helicopters.)

I don't know what school you went to, just that there was a brilliant music teacher, but I can't remember her name. I do know that, when you left school, you went to the music college and studied the flute. I don't think your parents were too pleased about that, even before you met Mum—they'd have preferred you to help them run the restaurant.

What else? I know that your father used to love a song about a galloping horseman. And that your favorite food was your mother's dumplings, called *nongjia jiaozi,* which you said meant "village dumplings." You taught me how to make them, and they are still my favorite food.

Not a lot to go on, really, is it? But anything would be better than where I've just come from. Aunt Sarah was all right, I suppose, though so cool and controlled that you'd never think she was the sister of warm, impulsive Mum. Maybe I could have found a way of handling Flo and Caitlin's spitefulness. I did love the birds, and I thought I liked Uncle John, until that morning I try not to think about.

Here comes the waitress with the shaved head and the nose ring. She's taken my teacup away. Does she think I ought to go? Should I order another tea? Maybe it would stop me from falling asleep.

I hope there won't be too many Chans in the phone book.

CHAN CONVERSATIONS

"Hello, is that Mrs. Chan?"

"Who's speaking?"

"It's . . . my name's Chan too. Um . . . I'm trying to do some research into my family tree and—"

"Where did you get my number?"

"From the phone book. It's just that—"

"I'm sorry, I can't help you."

*　　*　　*

"The number you have dialed has not been recognized."

*　　*　　*

"Hello, is that Mr. Chan?"

"Chah twing . . . (CRACKLE CRACKLE) . . . Chan . . . tsiu chong (CRACKLE CRACKLE) not here."

"I'm sorry, I didn't quite catch that. I'm looking for either Mr. or Mrs. Chan."

"Chah shing help you liu (CRACKLE CRACKLE) chong."

"I'm sorry, I can't understand what you're saying."

Click.

*　　*　　*

"Hello, I'm looking for my grandmother or my grandfather. Their surname's Chan."

"I don't think you've got the right number."

*　　*　　*

"Hello, is that Mrs. Chan?"

"Mrs. Chan, yes."

"I'm sorry if I've got the wrong number. I'm looking for the Mrs. Chan who used to own a Chinese restaurant."

"This not a restaurant, no."

"No, I know it's not a restaurant, but I wonder if you used to work in a restaurant."

"I think you got the wrong number. This not a restaurant."

ORCHESTRA ORPHAN MISSING

Leonora Watts-Chan, the fifteen-year-old whose musician parents were tragically killed in the June 8 "orchestra crash," has gone missing.

Leonora had been living in Bristol at the home of her mother's sister, Mrs. Sarah Baldwin.

"She seemed to have settled in so well, though of course she was devastated about losing both her parents," said Mrs. Baldwin. "She got on well with my two teenage daughters and was due to start school with them on Tuesday."

Leonora set off for the bus stop on September 10 with her two cousins, but then told them she had forgotten her PE kit and was going back to the house to fetch it. That was the last time anyone in the family saw her.

"I'll be fine."

Leonora did not appear at school, and later Mrs. Baldwin found a note saying that she was going to London to see old friends. The note ended, "I'll be fine. Don't worry."

Leonora was wearing the bottle-green school uniform of Bristol High School. She was carrying a black and turquoise Adidas bag containing her schoolbooks, which has not been found. Leonora is about 5 feet 2 inches, with short, dark hair and oriental features.

Mr. Barry Yates, a ticket clerk at Bristol Temple Meads Station, said that a girl answering Leonora's description bought a single ticket for Paddington on Tuesday morning.

"I remember her because she was quite chatty, although she seemed a bit nervous too," said Mr. Yates. "She said she was going to visit an art gallery. I didn't ask why she wasn't at school because I didn't think it was my business."

Leonora lived in North London before her parents were killed, and it is possible that she is staying with people she knew there. However, inquiries have so far drawn a blank. Anyone who thinks they may have seen Leonora should phone Missing People, 0500 700 700.

Finlay stirred the doughnut mixture and gazed absently out of the van. The Barras market bustled around him, but he barely noticed. He sighed a deep sigh.

"That's a long face for a Saturday," said Marina, scooping a doughnut out of the hot oil and dumping it onto the sugar tray. "Cheer up, it may never happen."

"It already has," said Finlay.

"What is it this time? School or Mum and Dad?"

"Both," said Finlay. "It's those bloody N of Ms."

"Language, Finlay!" Marina reproached him automatically. She turned the doughnut over in the sugar. "I thought N of M was a rock band," she said.

"That's Eminem, and he's a rapper," said Finlay. "N of M is short for Notification of Misconduct. They're these slips of paper the school gives you, and your parents have to sign them. Mum said if I got any more she'd stop this week's pocket money. Then I was late for school on Tuesday and got one. So I forged her signature."

"Finlay! This sounds like the slippery downward slope. Did the school swallow it?"

"Yes, but then on Wednesday one of the other paperboys was off and Rab gave me all these extra houses to do, so I was late again."

"And you got another Eminem?"

"N of M—no, but I would have. I couldn't face that, so I wrote a note from Mum saying I'd been to the dentist."

"Finlay! I wouldn't have given you this job if I'd known you were such a hardened criminal."

"Only the school went and phoned her," said Finlay bitterly.

"What gave you away? The handwriting, was it?"

"No, it was the *P*s," said Finlay. "Apparently there's only one in *apologize* and two in *appointment*. What a bloody stupid language."

"Language, Finlay!"

"That's what I just said—a bloody stupid one. So now that's the pocket money gone *and* Mum's going to stop me doing the paper round if I'm late again. I'll never get that guitar, and Ross'll probably find someone else to be in his band. It's so unfair."

Marina just laughed as she picked up some doughnuts with the tongs and transferred them to a polythene bag. "Five for a pound!" she yelled to the world in general, and then said to Finlay, "All this talk of *P*s has gone to my bladder. Mind the van a minute, can you, son?"

As soon as Marina had gone, it got busy. Finlay sold six bags of doughnuts. There was only one left; Marina would have to fry some more when she got back. Finlay was considered too young to be allowed to do the actual frying—another of life's unfairnesses.

A teenage girl with glossy black hair and a beige anorak

was hovering around the van. A bulky navy blue nylon bag was slung over her shoulder. She looked vaguely familiar to Finlay. Where had he seen her before? She backed away when she saw him looking at her, and a man with three runny-nosed kids came up to the van and ordered candy flosses. Whirling the pink fluffy strands around and around the sticks was something Finlay *was* trusted to do, and it was fun. He took five pounds from the man and turned to cash it.

When he turned back with the 50p change, he was just in time to see the girl in the beige anorak seize the last bag of doughnuts and run off with it.

"Hey! Stop!" In two strides, Finlay was at the van door. He jumped down and was after her. Through the candy floss kids, past a plant stall, around a corner. There she was, diving into a doorway! A second later and he'd have run on past. Instead, he swerved and charged in after her.

He found himself inside a vast low shed full of stalls selling ornaments, the kind of useless things his mother liked to collect. The girl dodged around a table covered in rearing china horses and past a huge brass gong that dangled from the ceiling. Finlay brushed against the gong and set it swinging gently. A man reached out and grabbed his arm.

"Slow down, you!" he said. Finlay wriggled out of his grasp and went on running, his eyes still on the girl. She had stopped by a tall, twisty hat stand and was looking around, searching frantically for a different exit. When her eyes met Finlay's, they filled with panic and she started off again. She ran around the edge of the building, heading for a door in the far corner.

I'll get there first, thought Finlay, spotting a narrow passageway between stalls, which led directly to the door. Old postcards, old prints, old books—Finlay ran past them all, gathering speed and swerving to avoid a fat man who was browsing over some old coins.

What happened next happened very quickly: a bumping of shoulders, a foot on a shoelace, a fall. Finlay was on the hard floor, his hands and knees smarting. A few other things seemed to be on the floor too—china things.

As Finlay scrambled to his feet, he caught a glimpse of the girl. She had reached the exit door and was disappearing through it. She was going to get away. But that was the least of Finlay's problems.

"Look what you've done!" an angry voice was saying. A woman with spiky orange hair was waving something in his face, or rather two things—two broken halves of a hideous purple seal. The fat man and the coin seller looked silently on, obviously enjoying the drama.

"I'm sorry," said Finlay. "Can you superglue it, maybe?"

It was the wrong thing to say.

"Superglue! I'll superglue *you* to the floor till you cough up thirty pounds for this piece."

"Thirty pounds!" Finlay repeated, aghast.

"That's what I said. And if those coronation mugs are broken, they'll cost you an extra twenty-five each." She put down the seal and picked up the two mugs, appearing disappointed to find that one was still intact but triumphant when she discovered the severed handle of the other.

"Running away from someone, were you?" She eyed him speculatively, as if uncertain whether to suspect him of theft or mugging.

"No, *after* someone. I do a Saturday job in the doughnut van, and this girl stole a bag of—"

But the woman didn't really want to know about any crime other than Finlay's. She thrust the broken china into a carrier bag. "Keep an eye on my stuff, will you—what's left of it," she said to the coin seller. Then, seizing Finlay's arm, she marched him back along the narrow passageway, toward daylight and doughnuts and Marina.

Marina. Finlay realized he wasn't looking forward to seeing her. But perhaps she would still be in the toilet . . . or perhaps she'd understand. . . .

She wasn't, and she didn't.

"*There* you are," she said. "This gentleman says you ran off with his change." The man who had bought the candy floss was standing there with his three kids. Their snot was now bright pink.

"Oh, no! Sorry. I didn't mean to." What had he done with the 50p? It had been in his hand when he saw the girl take the doughnuts. "I must have dropped it when I fell. I was trying to catch this thief, you see." But again no one seemed interested in his story.

"Don't worry, I've given the gentleman his money, but it's coming off today's wages, and they're the last wages you're getting," said Marina grimly. "Running off like that! Supposing someone had robbed the till while you were gone!"

"I *knew* he was up to no good," said the china seller, triumphant once again, and proceeded to tell Marina about the breakages. She produced the broken seal and mug. "If you're his mum, you owe me fifty-five pounds," she said.

"I'm not his mum—heaven forbid," said Marina, but surprisingly she put an arm around Finlay almost as if she were. "But fifty-five quid sounds a bit steep to me. I'd have thought you'd keep your valuable pieces locked up or at the back of the stall." She seemed to have taken against the other woman. Finlay listened to them haggling and waited in resignation for the moment when Marina would tell her his name and address.

But to his surprise, Marina was handing the woman a twenty-pound note. "That's for the mug," she said. "The seal looks like something left behind at a jumble sale, but I'll give you a pound for it."

The woman protested loudly but disappeared quite quickly with the money.

"Thanks, Marina—I'll pay it back out of my pocket money," said Finlay.

"I somehow doubt you'll be getting much pocket money with all these Eminems you keep getting," said Marina. "I'll take it out of the next couple of weeks' wages."

"But . . . I thought you said—"

"Aye, but I'm giving you another chance." The battle with the china seller seemed to have softened Marina's attitude to Finlay. "Now, tell me what happened, you daft wee bugger."

Finlay resisted the temptation to say, "Language, Marina!" and started to tell her about the girl with the glossy black hair and the beige anorak. And as he relived the moment when he'd noticed her hovering outside the van, he suddenly knew where he'd seen her before. It was in yesterday's *Sun*. ORCHESTRA ORPHAN MISSING.

LEO ▨ ▨ ▨ ▨
Hobnobbing

I can't get the swans quite right. This is my third sketch, and they still look more like geese. And of course they won't keep still. Now one of them is out of the water and is waddling right up to me.

No, you're not having one of my doughnuts, you greedy thing. I'm nearer to starving than you are. People are always feeding you. Look at that old lady with all the shopping bags; I bet one of them has got some crusts in it for you. What's she taking out? A whole loaf, it looks like. And another one! And all I've got is two measly doughnuts.

Yes, I know they're not my doughnuts, strictly speaking. I shouldn't have taken them, and I felt sorry for that kid running after me. He *was* just a kid, in spite of his tough-looking Goth gear. Probably doing a Saturday job, and he'll get into trouble now because of me. But my money's run out, and I was so hungry! Midnight Oil tea gets you through the night, but it's not exactly filling.

This bench by the pond has become a kind of home. I've only been in Glasgow four days, but I'm losing track of the number of naps I've had on it.

The swan is back with the others, gobbling up the old lady's bread. There must be about a hundred slices in the water. She's turned her back on them now, and she's walking toward me. No, don't come and sit on this bench—it's mine! Why can't you find another one?

"That's a nice picture," she says as she sits down beside me.

I smile and close the sketchbook. I don't want to get into a conversation with her.

"Have you got the time, hen?" she asks.

"Yes"—but as I glance at my watch, the thought crosses my mind that I should sell it, or pawn it, to raise some extra cash. "It's twenty-five past two."

She nods, pleased by my answer. "Ronnie'll be out for his Accompanied at half past."

"Oh." I haven't the faintest idea what she's talking about.

"They willnae give him Unaccompanied. The Godfather gets Unaccompanied, but Ronnie jist gets Accompanied."

If I look baffled, she doesn't notice. The words keep coming nonstop, like the slices of bread she's just been throwing into the pond.

"Aye, the Godfather gets Unaccompanied, but no' Ronnie—he'd do a runner if they gave him Unaccompanied. There's that many pubs 'round here. It's alcohol-induced wi' Ronnie. If Ronnie could stay off the bevvy, he'd be as right as you are, hen."

She rummages in one of her bags and holds out a packet of biscuits to me. I take one and try to hand the packet back, but she waves it away.

"Keep it, hen. I've got another one for Ronnie, and one for the Godfather. Jim disnae like biscuits. I've got some crisps and juice for Jim. Whit's your name, then?"

"Leo," I reply automatically, and then wish I hadn't. I'm not supposed to be Leo Watts-Chan anymore. 'Specially not since yesterday's papers and that picture of me with "Leo, the Orchestra Orphan" underneath. Just when I was beginning to think I'd escaped the papers. Just when I was telling myself that there are dozens of runaway homeless teenagers; no one wants to read about yet another one. But the plane crash is still fresh in people's minds, so I'm news.

The name doesn't seem to ring a bell with this lady, thank goodness—or rather, it does, but a different one.

"I'm a Leo," she says. "Fiery and generous, that's me." She rummages again and produces a newspaper. My heart stops for a second. Maybe she *has* recognized me.

But it's a local paper, with a headline about a corrupt councillor. In any case, she's not interested in the news; she flicks through to the horoscope page and reads out, "Leo. A chance encounter can affect your home life."

She nudges me. "A chance encounter. That willnae be Ronnie. Ronnie's planned. It must be you, pal!" She laughs, then points at two men, one small and one burly, coming along the path toward us. "Here's Ronnie! Here he comes! And that's Jim Docherty with him." She waves at them wildly.

"Move up, hen." She squeezes up to me and pats at the empty space on the bench.

"Hiya, Mary," says the burly man. The small one smiles and says nothing, but it is into his hands that Mary thrusts the packet of biscuits. He must be Ronnie.

"Chocolate Hob Nobs—your favorite, Ronnie," says the burly man. Ronnie's smile widens, but he still doesn't speak. He doesn't sit down on the bench either, but shuffles from foot to foot. There is a glazed look in his eyes.

"This is my new wee friend," says Mary, indicating me. "She's a Leo like me. Fiery and generous, aren't we, hen?"

As if to prove her own generosity, she picks up a bag and holds it out to big Jim.

"Biscuits fur the Godfather, Irn-Bru and crisps fur you, Jim," she says.

Jim shakes his head and sighs but takes the bag. "You're spoiling us, Mary," he says.

"Aye, but I can afford to. I didnae spend my DLA all at once—not like last time."

Jim rolls his eyes at me. Then he glances at my sketchbook. "Are you from Mary's painting class?" he asks.

I am saved from answering by Mary. "I've stopped going to that painting class, Jim. I didnae like it. There was a wumman there kept giving me looks."

"You should go, Mary. You don't want to hang around here all day. Why don't you ask your CPN if there's any other classes?"

CPN? DLA? Accompanied and Unaccompanied? What is this world I've stumbled into?

Mary shakes her head and turns to little Ronnie, who is still shuffling from foot to foot. "How's the pool going, pal? Still beating the Godfather?"

Ronnie nods and smiles his glazed smile.

"You're giving him too much of they pills, Jim," says Mary, and suddenly I get the picture. Ronnie is a patient, a mental patient probably; so presumably is the man she calls the Godfather. The hospital must be very near here, and Jim must be one of the nurses, taking Ronnie for his daily accompanied stroll. Where does Mary fit in? Has she been in hospital too? Is that how she knows them all?

"Come on, then, Ronnie," says Jim. "Say good-bye to Mary." It is as if he's talking to a child. Ronnie waves to Mary, Jim takes his arm, and the pair of them carry on along the path.

I feel sorry for Mary. She'd been looking forward so much to seeing Ronnie, but their meeting has only lasted for a few minutes and he didn't say anything. What will she do now?

And what will I do? Say good-bye too and go in search of a more peaceful bench to sleep on?

"Will you take a wee cup of tea, hen?" asks Mary.

To my surprise, I find myself accepting. I thrust the sketchbook back into the hold-all, which I'm so sick of lugging around everywhere. "Let me carry some of your bags," I say, and take a couple with my free hand. They're much heavier than I expected.

Mary laughs.

"Cat food!" she says.

Missing People

"Hello, you're through to Missing People."

"Oh, hi . . . er, I've seen the girl that's gone missing."

"Can you give us the name of the missing person, please?"

"That one in the paper."

"We do have several thousand missing people in our files. We need to work from a name."

"I'm sorry, I can't remember. It wasn't my paper, see. I just deliver them. But it was yesterday she was in it. She's kind of Chinesy looking."

"Do you mean Leonora Watts-Chan?"

"Aye, that was it. I'm sure it was her. She nicked a bag of doughnuts from my van. Well, it's not my van, really, it's—"

"Can I just take down a few details first, please? What's your name?"

"Finlay Grant."

"And your address?"

"Fifty-eight Tiverton Road."

"Where is that?"

"It's in Glasgow. . . . But you won't write to me, will you? I don't want you to write. My parents don't know about this, see. I broke some stuff when I was chasing after the girl, and I don't want them to find out. Is there a reward, by the way? I don't mind you writing to me if there's a reward."

"**Finlay!**"

"Oh, no. That's my dad. I'll have to be quick."

"Can you tell me when and where you think you saw the girl?"

"Yes, it was at the Barras this morning."

"The barrows, did you say?"

"No, the Barras. It's a market. She nicked a bag of dough-nuts and ran off. I nearly lost my job because of her."

"Can you remember what she was wearing?"

"It was some kind of anorak. Light colored. I think it had a hood. She had a great big bag too."

"Was it a school bag?"

"No, not really."

"**Finlay! Stop hogging that phone!**"

"Can you describe it? Hello? Hello . . . ?"

"**You know Mum's expecting a call.**"

"Sorry, Dad."

"**Who were you calling anyway?**"

"Ross. It was about the physics homework."

LEO
Flat 2/1

The tabby cat is sitting on my lap, purring like a road drill.

"Midget likes you," says Mary.

"*Midget*? But she's enormous."

28

"Aye, but she was a wee toty thing when I found her. She was in the back court, sniffing around by the bins. All skin and bones, she was—a wee toty thing."

I have the feeling that Mary collects waifs and strays, "wee toty things," and that I'm the latest one.

"My cousins used to call *me* Midget," I tell her.

"That's no' very nice."

"They called me a lot worse things than that." I stroke the cat rhythmically, and it seems to have an effect not just on her purr (which gets even louder) but on my own voice. I find myself telling her all about Flo and Caitlin and how they were always taunting me—"just joking" as they called it—about my clothes and my height and my eyes and my skin. "We never really got on, even before I went to live there. Maybe it all started with our mums: They were sisters but not at all alike. Aunt Sarah was a beautician, and she was always immaculate looking, with manicured fingernails and high-heeled shoes, and Mum was . . . well, a bit unconventional."

"A bit of a tearaway, was she?"

"Yes, I suppose so. I think maybe Aunt Sarah disapproved of her and Dad not being married. Not as much as Dad's parents did, though. They cut him off when he moved in with Mum."

"That's harsh, that is."

"I know. I don't think Dad ever forgave them, although he did try to explain it to me: He said that, in the Chinese community, anything like that was completely taboo. You didn't even go out with someone unless you were definitely going to get married."

"Could they no get married just to please his ma and da?"

"That's what I sometimes think. But my dad could be quite stubborn too. Anyway, they didn't—they moved to London to join orchestras. And then they had me. Mum called me Leonora after a Beethoven overture. That was so typical of her. Apparently my first bed was a spare cello case."

"She played the cello then, aye?"

"Yes, but in a different orchestra from Dad. They never went on tour at the same time, so that there would always be one of them around to look after me. But then, just three months ago, Dad's orchestra was invited to Spain and they needed some extra cellos for a particular piece. It was one of Mum's favorite pieces—by some Spanish composer, for a singer and twelve cellos. I said she should go: I could stay with Aunt Sarah and Uncle John. I even pretended I felt okay about Flo and Caitlin. So Mum said 'Just this once.'"

"And was it?"

"Yes." I pause a second and watch my hand stroking the cat. It's hard to go on, even though I want to. My voice falters as I say the words: "Yes, it was, because the plane crashed, and everyone was killed."

I hate telling people that. It's always such a shock to

them, and I find myself trying to comfort them when it should really be the other way around.

But Mary takes grief in her stride. Her eyes soften, and she pats my arm with a bony hand. "So you're the wee orchestra orphan? I read about you when it happened. Poor wean." She passes me the chocolate Hob Nobs.

"What about your uncle?" she asks. "Was he as bad as the others?"

"I used to like him when I was little. I thought I did, anyway. Maybe it was his birds I liked, really. He keeps all these birds—about twenty of them."

"Pigeons, are they? Wee puddie-doos?"

"No, budgies and canaries, mostly. And some cockatiels too. I've got some pictures of them here."

I reach down for my bag. Midget jumps off my lap and then straight back again once the sketchbook is open on the table.

"They're good, they are," says Mary. "You're a good artist. You're Leo da Vinci, you are!"

I don't flick back to the pictures of Mum and Dad. I don't think I could bear to look at those just now. I stick to the bird ones.

"These were my two favorites," I say, turning the page to the picture of the two lemon-yellow cockatiels with the bright orange spots on their cheeks. "They were called Clemmy and Lemmy."

She chuckles. "The wee rascals. Did they talk, aye?"

"Not that I ever heard, but Uncle John talked to them all the time. He kept them in the spare room. Their cages took up nearly half the room—he'd built all these shelves for them. That was the room I slept in when I went to live there."

"Did the birds no' keep you awake?"

"No, because he'd rigged up a curtain across the cages to stop the light getting through. I liked sharing with the birds—at first anyway. I liked sketching them. The social worker wasn't happy, though."

"Are they ever? Don't get me started about social workers," says Mary.

I don't give her the chance—I'm quite keen to keep going myself. It's such a relief to be able to share all this with someone at last. "She said it was against the law and I could get some disease off the birds, but I was just glad not to be sharing with Flo and Caitlin."

"Aye, the wee witches?"

"Not so wee. Flo's fifteen like me, and Caitlin's thirteen. Actually, Flo could be all right when she was on her own. Caitlin was the worst. She even pretended she had to make a list of all the words meaning yellow for her English holiday homework. She kept going 'round the house saying 'I know—jaundiced!' and 'I've got another one—sulfur!' Aunt Sarah actually believed her and signed the list on the last day of the holidays."

"I'd have slapped her 'round the face if she was my

wean," says Mary. I feel a bit shocked. I can't imagine friendly, generous Mary being violent even to her worst enemy.

"That was last Monday," I continue. "I was supposed to be starting at their school the next day, but I ran away instead."

"Did they have a gang then, aye? Were they going to bully you?"

"Oh, it wasn't *them* I was running away from, not really. It was Uncle John."

"The bird man?"

"Yes."

The next bit is going to be harder to tell. I pause and stop stroking Midget. She lifts her head and opens her eyes reproachfully, till I carry on with the stroking and the story.

"Uncle John used to bring me in a cup of tea in the mornings, and then he'd draw the curtain across the cages to wake up the birds. This would be quite early—about seven o'clock, even earlier sometimes, but I didn't mind that. I quite liked drinking my tea in bed and watching the birds. Sometimes the tea would be a bit cold, but I just thought he'd been pottering about and had forgotten to bring it in to me. He was a bit absentminded like that. But one morning I woke up and . . . he was kneeling on the floor by my bed. He was just kneeling there, leaning over me and staring at me. Usually he wears glasses, those magnifying kind, but he hadn't got them on, and his brown eyes were just inches away from my face. They looked smaller without the glasses, and all watery. It was so creepy. Of course then he started rummaging around under the bed, pretending he'd lost a packet of birdseed or something, but I knew he hadn't."

"Did you tell your auntie?"

"No. I didn't know what to say. I didn't think she'd believe me anyway. And then I started wondering if it had really happened—until it happened again a few days later."

"Tried to mess about with you, did he?"

"No—no, he didn't actually touch me or anything. Just knelt there staring with his little watery eyes. The second time he didn't do the 'whoops, I've lost the birdseed' routine, though. He just gave me this sort of soppy smile for a few seconds and then went and fetched my tea. He'd put it down on the table by the cages, and it was getting cold. He'd probably been staring at me for ages. Maybe he'd been doing it *every morning*. It was such a horrible thought."

"What did you do—throw the tea in his face?"

"No. It was stupid, really. I just whispered 'thanks,' like I usually did. And after that, when it kept happening, it felt too late to say anything. I suppose I should have told him to get out or something, but . . . well, it was his house and his room and his birds, and . . . it's not as if he'd actually *done* anything. Looking's not a crime, or is it? Anyway, he did get out without me telling him to, but he still had that stupid, soft kind of smile on his face. It was as if he was sharing a secret with me."

"I'll wipe that smile off his face if I ever see him," says Mary. "I'll get the Godfather to wipe it off, so I will. The dirty old man."

"I hope you never do see him. He thinks I'm in London. But the thing is, I still didn't know if he *was* a dirty old man. It felt like it was me that had the dirty mind, being so horrible and suspicious. Maybe Uncle John just felt sorry for me, you know, being an orphan—maybe he felt fatherly or something. I was so confused. It's not like I had any friends in Bristol that I could talk to. I did used to phone Bridget sometimes—she's my best friend in London—but she was on holiday when it started happening. Anyway, it wasn't the sort of thing you chat about on the phone, somehow. I suppose I should have told the social worker." (Mary snorts—she definitely doesn't think much of social workers.) "But instead I came here. I thought it would be easy to track down my grandparents, only it's not."

I tell her about the twenty-two Chans in the phone book and how hopeless it has been trying to phone them. "I didn't pack my mobile because I thought people might somehow trace me that way. So I have to use phone boxes, but I keep running out of change. And then everyone sounds so suspicious! Half of them put the phone down before I've got going, and some of them never pick it up in the first place."

"You'd be better going to their houses," says Mary.

"Yes, that's what I decided. I copied all the addresses out of the phone book, and I bought an *A–Z* of Glasgow. But now I feel too scared."

"Why? They willnae bite your head off."

"It's not that. It's because my picture was in yesterday's *Sun*."

Mary gasps, suitably impressed. "You'll want to lie low for a wee while, then," she says.

"But where? I can't afford to go to that café anymore. My money's run out. I'm so tired, and I feel so dirty!" The tears that wouldn't come when I was telling Mary about Mum and Dad come now, and I can't stop them.

"I just want a bath!" I cry. And suddenly I can see our bathroom back home—a tiny room made even tinier by Mum's enormous cheese plant. Dad and I used to call it the Beanstalk. I want desperately to be in that bathroom. I want to be squeezing a spot in the mirror and for Mum to come in and tell me that I'll only make it worse.

My jerky sobs cause Midget to turn her head in concern.

"You can have a bath, hen," says Mary. "And you can have a bed too."

Here you are, nice clean water. That's what you like, isn't it? Oh, look, nasty husks—let's take them away. Nice new seeds. Yes, you like the stripy ones, don't you, Clemmy? Let Lemmy have some too. Who's a pretty girl, then? You are! Don't you want to play with your bell? Are you missing our little friend? Daddy's missing her too. On you hop. That's right. Don't be shy. Don't be sad. She'll be back. Daddy's going to find her.

FINLAY ░░░
Canal

"Is that the new school crest, then?" asked Rab, pointing at Finlay's back. Finlay was wearing the Breakneck hoodie he'd been given for his thirteenth birthday. "Very good— Breakneck! I suppose that's what the staff do to the kids, or is it the other way 'round?"

Finlay was deciding whether it would be more dignified to ignore this wit or to enlighten Rab on the subject of his favorite band when the phone in the depot rang.

Rab's mirth vanished.

"What? Not again!" he said. The force with which he

slammed the receiver down jolted the cigarette in his other hand and sprinkled ash all over the phone.

"Bloody hell! That wee wimp Ross McGovern gets more colds than I get hot dinners. Who's going to do Glennie Avenue?"

The few remaining paperboys headed for the door hastily, but Finlay wasn't quick enough. Rab clamped a hand on his shoulder. "Not so fast, pal! I've got a present for you." He thrust a bundle of extra papers into Finlay's bag.

"I can't! It's not fair! I'll be late for school," complained Finlay.

"I'll break their necks if they break yours," Rab offered, and then, more helpfully, "and I'll run you to Glennie Avenue."

In fact, Glennie Avenue was surprisingly quick to do. As Finlay took a short cut back along the canal to his regular route he calculated how much he would earn if he did an extra paper run every morning. It would help to make up for the two weeks' wages he'd lost at the Barras.

Finlay still seethed when he thought about the dough-nut thief. It wouldn't be so bad if the Missing People phone line had taken him seriously, but it seemed they hadn't. The day after he made the call, Finlay had read in the *Sun* that there had been "dozens of alleged sightings of Leonora Watts-Chan" and that police were follow-ing several leads in the London area and another in Bournemouth—no mention of Glasgow.

That was last week. Since then, another body had been found in a bin and the orchestra orphan story seemed to have fizzled out.

Finlay kicked an Irn-Bru can along the canal towpath and then stamped on it. Startled, a brown bird with a red beak swam out from the bank, rippling the glinting water of the canal. Finlay stopped and watched the wobbly reflections of some tall nettles and a tree with orange berries. It was peaceful here, and the late September sunshine was surprisingly warm for the time of day. Typical, thought Finlay. It rains all holidays, and then once school starts, it's sunny for weeks on end.

Thinking of school, he set off again, but then stopped. Ahead of him, across the canal, was a narrow swing bridge, and on it sat a girl in a white T-shirt. She had her back to him, and she was looking down into the water. Then Finlay saw that she had a pad of paper on her lap and was sketching. The girl's hair was short, dark, and glossy, just like the doughnut girl's hair. It couldn't actually be her, could it? No, he had her on his mind, that was all. But then he noticed that she was sitting on a pale-colored anorak. That didn't prove anything either, yet Finlay felt his heart beat faster.

What should he do? He could creep up on her and get a good look at her face. But then she'd see him and run. If it was the doughnut girl, she was a fast runner, and Finlay wasn't—especially not with his bag full of papers. She would just get away again, and then what? If he rang the Missing People brigade, they probably wouldn't be any more impressed than they were last time. Unless . . . yes, that was it! Finlay didn't have a camera, but Mum did, and it would only take a couple of minutes to nip home for it. He turned around and walked quietly till he reached the gap in the hedge. When he was through it, he ran.

"That was quick!" said Mum. "You'll be on time for once."

"I haven't finished yet," said Finlay. "But, Mum, I need to borrow your camera."

"What for?"

"I want to take some photos of the canal. It's for our art project."

"But why now? Shouldn't you finish your paper round? Can't you do it this evening?"

"No, the light won't be right. Oh, go on, Mum, please."

"Well. . . ." Finlay waited for her to start up about the two mobile phones he'd lost this year, but instead she said, "Oh, all right, then." She was doing her best to sound grudging but was actually pleased to discover this new artistic streak in Finlay.

"Thanks, Mum." The camera was hanging from a coat hook in the hall. Finlay took it and ran.

He reached the hedge by the canal and peered around it. There was no one on the swing bridge. He was too late.

But no! There she was, farther down the towpath, walking swiftly away from him, her sketchbook tucked under her arm. Instead of following her along the path, Finlay decided to stay on the other side of the hedge on the road, which ran parallel to the canal. He crossed the road so that she'd be less likely to see or hear him through the hedge. If he timed it right, he could rejoin the towpath at the next bridge before the girl got there. But first he must remember how Mum's camera worked. He took it out of its case and pointed it at a car. It was simple enough—look through this window, click this button—yes, that was it.

A man getting into another car gave him a suspicious look. Finlay ignored him and ran, probably making the man even more suspicious, but that was too bad.

Past the bus stop, past the mini supermarket. There it was, the next opening to the canal. Would he reach it before she did? The hedge was too thick here for him to see through it.

He stopped running, poised the camera, and stepped out onto the canal path. He looked right—no one. He looked left and found himself almost face-to-face with her. And it *was* her.

Click!

The girl's eyes widened as she recognized him. Finlay wasn't prepared for what happened next. She grabbed the camera and ran.

"Stop! Stop! That's my mum's camera!"

Finlay ran after her, through another gap in the hedge,

along Endred Close and then right into Struan Drive. She dived into the entrance to a block of flats. Finlay followed. You're cornered now, he thought. These were the flats he delivered papers to, and he knew that there wasn't another way out.

He clattered up the stairs after her. As he reached the second-floor landing, he was just in time to see her let herself into a door. Finlay knew the door well. It was McNally 2/1.

LEO
Face-to-Face

"Hiya, Leo, hen! Did you do some nice pictures, aye?" Mary greets me. Then, "What is it?" as she sees the panic on my face.

"Shh, Mary! Someone's seen me." I beckon her into the bedroom, the room farthest from the front door. "He's there outside—he's on the landing!"

"Who is? It's no' the bird man, is it?" Mary's eyes are glittering, her voice a stage whisper.

"No, it's that boy. . . . I'm sure it's him—the one I told you about, the one from the doughnut van."

The doorbell rings. "That's him! Why did I run here? Now I'm trapped!"

"We willnae let him in."

"But I've got his camera, Mary! He took a photo of me, and I just grabbed it. . . . Oh, what shall I do?"

Another ring, longer, louder, and a rapping of the letter box. I clutch Mary's arm. It's bony through her thin, flowery blouse. She pats my hand in reassurance, but her bright eyes look wild.

"Open the door! I know you're there!" comes the boy's voice. And then, louder, "Open the door, or I'll call the police."

He means it too. What can we do?

Mary is suddenly decisive. She points to the large old-fashioned wardrobe. "Get in there, hen! I'll stop his blethering."

The wardrobe is full of Mary's charity-shop dresses and blouses. The musty-smelling nylon is cool against my face in the darkness. I can hear her voice coming from the hallway.

"Will you stop that carry on!" she says. But now she's laughing. Why?

"I spy with my little eye!" She must be looking through the little spy hole in the front door. "It's my wee paperboy all the time. Can ye no' put it through the letter box, son?"

I can't make out the boy's reply, but then Mary says, "No, wee man, there's only me—me and the moggie. . . . No, there's nae lassie here. You've got the wrong house."

"She *is* here! I *saw* her! She's got my mum's camera!" The voice is louder now, much too loud for my liking.

"Jist gie me my *Morning Post* and stop blethering. You'll be late for school."

"I'm not going to school. I'm going to the police station!"

"Aye, and I'll go with you and tell them you've been causing a breach of the peace."

Mary is keeping up the act, but I know it's no good. The boy means business. And if he carries on at this volume, everyone in the flats will find out about me.

I push open the wardrobe door and call to Mary, "You'd better let him in. I'll give him his camera back."

The camera, but not the photograph. It's an old-fashioned camera, not a digital one. As Mary fiddles with the chain on the door, I fiddle with the camera. *Click,* open, close. Now the film is exposed, and the picture will be ruined.

"Where is she? And where's my camera?" comes the boy's voice. Mary has let him in. He's in the hall. Feeling something like stage fright, I open the bedroom door and make my entrance.

The boy spins around. We're face-to-face—for the third time.

"Is it him, aye? Is it the doughnut boy?" asks Mary.

"No—*she's* the doughnut *girl*!" says the boy. "She stole my doughnuts, and now she's got my mum's camera. Give it back, you thief!"

I hand him the camera. "Here you are, but stop spying on me."

"I'd rather be a spy than a thief."

"Stop calling me a thief!"

"Well, you are one. I nearly lost my job because of you, and now I've got to pay for those ornaments."

"I don't know what you're on about. I didn't steal any ornaments."

"Maybe not, but you're still a thief. Stealing things and running away all the time." A new idea strikes him. "I bet that's why you ran away in the first place, isn't it? I bet you stole stuff from your aunt and uncle!"

I can feel the blood draining from my face. So he does know. He knows who I am.

"What do you mean? *I'm* her auntie," Mary lies valiantly, but the boy's not swallowing it.

"You're not! You're not the one that was in the paper anyway." He turns on me again. "I recognized you the first time I saw you," he says, "and now I'm going to get the reward."

"No . . . listen . . . you don't understand." My voice feels as weak as my knees. It trails out.

"*You're* the one who doesn't understand," he shouts. "You just go 'round stealing things, not caring how other people feel. How do you think I'd feel if I lost my job? How do you think my mum would feel if her camera was stolen? My dad gave her that camera for Christmas."

Before I can answer, Mary turns on him. "Your da! Your ma! You're lucky to have a da and a ma. How d'ye think this wean feels? She's got no da and no ma—all she's got is an auntie who's a snob and an uncle who's a pervert and two nasty wee cousins."

The boy looks taken aback. Mary seizes her advantage. "She didnae want your ma's camera. She jist disnae want her photie splashed in all the papers. But you widnae think about that, wid ye? Ye'd have her back wi' that perverted bird man, is that it?"

"I'm sorry . . . I didn't know—"

"No, and you didnae think, neither. Christmas, you're on about! Christmas! What about the poor wee lassie? No ma, no da—what sort of Christmas do you think she's going to have?"

Mary's really in her stride now, and I'm beginning to feel sorry for the boy. He looks embarrassed; he's fingering his luminous yellow bag of newspapers. Now he's turning to the door.

"All right. I won't tell anyone. I'd better go."

But just as he reaches for the handle, there comes a light tap and a voice from the other side.

"Is everything all right, Miss McNally?"

"It's Dressing Gown," mutters the boy, and as abruptly as Mary began her tirade, she ends it with a hoot of laughter.

"Dressing Gown! Aye, it's Dressing Gown! I'm fine, Dressing Gown!" she yells. "Never better! How's yerself, Dressing Gown?"

"I'll be fine if you can just keep the noise down," comes the voice, huffy now.

Mary shrieks with laughter again: All the excitement seems to have gone to her head.

The boy looks a bit alarmed and catches my eye.

"Why don't you sit down, Mary? I'll make you a cup of tea," I suggest. It seems mean to leave the boy out. "Do you want some?"

"Aye, of course he does—don't you, wee man?" says Mary. Her aggression has been transformed into generosity now that we are all somehow allies against Dressing Gown. "And I know what he'll be wanting as well—chocolate Hob Nobs!"

TALKING TO THE BIRDS ▨ ▨ ▨
2

Wakey wakey. Look what Daddy's got you. A special treat. Chickweed. Oh, dear, are we all ruffled? You didn't like it in that van, did you? No, nasty van. Never mind. It's all right here, really. We'll get used to it. We don't care about the others anyway, do we? We'll be all right on our own. Yes, that's Chirpy's perch. Chirpy chirpy, perchie perchie! Look in your mirror. You're pretty, aren't you? There's nothing wrong with looking. Daddy was only looking. He was waiting for the bus, just like those silly girls. Whoops—it's gone in your water. Silly Daddy to put the water under Chirpy's perch. Silly Daddy!

Finlay took his English file and his copy of *Macbeth* out of the black bag with the skull patch on it. He nudged his teacup to one side of Mary's wobbly dining table and the plate of Jammie Dodgers to the other. (After a few heavy hints dropped over the last few days, Mary had finally realized that he preferred Jammie Dodgers to chocolate Hob Nobs.)

Leo leaned over Finlay's shoulder as he opened the file. "Are you sure you're okay about helping me again?" he asked her. "It's just I've got a bit behind—"

"I know. Too busy taking photos and catching criminals. No, it's fine. I love Shakespeare."

"You sound just like Ailsa Coutts."

"Who's she?"

"She's this girl in my class who understands all the *thee*s and *thou*s. She keeps blabbing on about what motivates Lady Macbeth. Our English teacher loves her."

"Why don't you get her to help you, then?" Leo sounded a touch offended.

"No, she wouldn't bother with a loser like me."

"Oh, so I'm second best, then?"

"No, you're dead good at explaining things."

"All right, then." Mollified, Leo seized the book. "Where have you got up to? Has Macbeth killed the king yet?"

"Yes, and now he's just had this other guy bumped off—you know, his friend Banquet."

Leo laughed, and Mary let out a wild cackle. "Banquet! That's a good name. How do you do, Banquet? Sit doon, Banquet—have a cup of tea."

"It's not banquet—it's Banquo," said Leo gently.

"Sorry, I was getting mixed up. We've been doing the banqueting scene."

"Oh, that's a great scene."

"It is if you don't have to write an essay about it." Finlay read aloud the heading he had scrawled at the top of the file paper: "Is Banquo's Ghost Meant to Be Real?"

"Well, what do you think?"

"Of course he's real," said Finlay. "Shakespeare says so. Look, it says here, 'Enter Banquo's ghost and sits in Macbeth's place.'"

"But don't you think that's really meant to be happening in Macbeth's mind?" said Leo.

"Aye," chipped in Mary. "It's like wi' Ronnie on Ward 7. One time he saw this chimney sweep talking to him oot the telly, but the telly wasnae on. There's that much funny stuff going on in people's heids."

"That's right," said Leo. "After all, no one else can see the ghost, and remember what Lady Macbeth says: 'You look but on a chair.'"

Finlay felt doubly annoyed. Not only did Leo seem to know the play off by heart, but she obviously thought that old Mary—who obviously hadn't even read it—had a better grasp of it than he had.

"I suppose you always come top in English, like Ailsa Coutts," he said.

"No, I don't," said Leo. "As a matter of fact, I don't even go to school."

"I know you don't anymore, but I mean . . . well, before—"

"I never did. I was home-educated. Mum and Dad used to take me to see a lot of plays and then we'd talk and talk about them."

"Oh," said Finlay. He never knew what to say when Leo mentioned her parents. Maybe he'd better get back to *Macbeth*.

"So you think Macbeth's a bit mental, then?" he said. "I think that's what Lady Macbeth thinks too. She says something about how he often has these fits and how everyone should take no notice and just get on with the banquet."

Mary cackled again. "Take no notice and get on wi' the banquet! That's good advice, that is! I'll tell that to Ronnie and the Godfather. Take no notice and get on wi' the banquet!"

Leo smiled, then turned back to Finlay. "But don't you see? Lady Macbeth just says that about Macbeth having fits to cover up for him. She's trying to put the guests off the scent. Macbeth doesn't really have fits. The real reason he sees the ghost is because he feels so guilty. I mean, he's just murdered his friend. Think how you'd feel if you'd murdered . . . well, me, for example."

"Aye, say you'd killed her after she'd taen your dough-nuts!" Mary was getting into the spirit of this argument. "You'd feel guilty then, wouldn't you, wee man?"

"No I wouldn't—it would serve her right!" said Finlay, and they all laughed. But underneath the laughter, Finlay realized that he *did* have a faintly guilty feeling about Leo. Why should that be? As she had more or less said, they were friends now, not enemies, and she had helped him with his homework for the last two days. So where did that guilty feeling come from? Finlay tried to push it to the back of his mind.

Mary was still laughing. Why did she laugh so much? "Take no notice and get on wi' the banquet!" she crowed yet again, thumping Finlay on the back. "Aye, let's have a banquet. Let's get in a Chinky!"

Finlay didn't think you were supposed to call a Chinese takeaway a "Chinky." It was what his English teacher and his mum would call "politically incorrect," especially when there was a real Chinese—well, half Chinese—person in the room. But Leo didn't seem to mind. At least, not about that.

"Listen, Mary, you can't keep spending your money on us like this," she said. "You've already bought me those clothes, and all those lovely oil pastels."

But Mary was flapping a leaflet about gleefully. "I've just got my DLA, and I'll spend it how I like. I'll spend it on a banquet!" she said. She picked up the phone.

"What's DLA?" Finlay whispered to Leo.

"Disability Living Allowance," Leo told him. "It's this money she gets every month from the government."

"One sparerib special, one sweet and sour king prawn, one chicken with ginger and pineapple, one beef in oyster sauce . . ." Mary seemed to be ordering the whole menu.

"We've got to stop her," said Leo.

But Finlay's mind had leapt in a different direction. "Hey—that restaurant could be the one your gran and granddad run," he said. Excited, he gripped Mary's arm. "Ask them if they're called Chan!" he mouthed.

Mary, catching the excitement, interrupted the flow of her order. "What are you? Chans? No? Sure there's no Chans lurking in the sweet and sour? You fish them out if there are—my wee girl here is looking for her granny and grandpa."

"I've just had a thought there," said Finlay, when Mary had at last put the phone down. "We could order food from a different place each week and ask each one the Chan question. That way we can track Leo's grandparents down without anyone sussing us out."

Mary clapped her hands. "You're our Sherlock Holmes!" she cried.

But Leo looked doubtful. "That would take ages. There must be loads of Chinese restaurants in Glasgow."

"Let's see." Finlay reached for Mary's Yellow Pages. "Here we are—Restaurants, Chinese," he said, and then, "You're right," as his finger ran down the long column. "There's fifty-six."

"So one a week would take over a year," said Leo. "Anyway, I don't even know if they've still got a restaurant."

But Mary was undaunted. "Sherlock! He's our Sherlock!" she said. "Hand over the book, Sherlock! We don't need to wait a week. Let's try this one—the Amber Wok. I bet they do a good banquet."

"Mary, *no!*" Leo tried to grab the phone. "We're going to have far too much food as it is."

"We're having a banquet!" said Mary. She still held the phone, but her expression changed. "We just need some mair guests," she said.

LEO
The Banquet

There are five of them. Five extra guests at the banquet.

Lorraine is the first to arrive. She's a lot younger than Mary, probably in her late twenties. She's been 'round here a few times before, though I don't feel I know her, as she doesn't speak often, and when she does, it is in a slow, dull voice. I haven't asked how she fits into Mary's life. Maybe they met in hospital. As usual, Lorraine is sitting slumped on the sofa, chain-smoking. That sofa is my bed, but I'm hardly in a position to complain.

The other four guests arrive together. Three of them are men, and one is a dog.

I recognize Ronnie straightaway. He is the quiet, shuffling man Mary gave the chocolate Hob Nobs to in the park the day I first met her. He sits down in a corner of the room, his knees touching his chin, and takes a can of beer out of one of the two carrier bags he has brought with him.

Mary pays more attention to the two older men. "It's the President and the Godfather!" she cries. "The reunited ones! The long-lost twins!"

"You're off your heid, Mary," says the one she calls the President. He has long, greasy hair, a stubbly chin, and a shabby leather jacket. "We're not long-lost. The Godfather's just been in Ward 7 for six months. They let him out yesterday."

"They've turned the key! They've set the leader free!" says Mary.

She's talked such a lot about the Godfather, and I'd been imagining a don't-mess-with-me Mafioso figure, but in fact he looks quite respectable, clean-shaven, with a short-back-and-sides haircut.

Mary grabs one of my hands and one of Finlay's. She

holds them up as if the three of us were about to take a bow at the theater. "This is Leo da Vinci. She's an artist. And Sherlock's a detective," she announces.

"I'm delighted to make your acquaintance," says the Godfather solemnly. Then he starts to hand the foil take-away containers 'round, murmuring polite but rather odd things like "I can assure you the chop suey is uncontaminated" and "It is perfectly in order to combine chicken with bamboo shoots." After that, he lapses into silence.

But if Lorraine, Ronnie, and the Godfather are quiet, the President and the dog make up for them.

The dog is handsome, black, silky, and badly behaved. I'm not sure which of the three men he belongs to, and he himself doesn't think he belongs to anyone. He began by chasing Mary's cat, Midget, who fled into the bedroom. Now he is roaming the sitting room, barking at anyone who is holding a sparerib.

The President eats with his fingers, only occasionally licking them clean. He talks even more than Mary, while still managing to wolf down large quantities of food. With his mouth full of king prawns, he tells us about all the countries he has been to, which according to him is just about every one in the world.

"Have you been to Egypt?" Finlay asks. "My mum and dad are planning to go on a Nile cruise."

"I lived in Egypt for years," says the President. "I know the Nile like the back of my hand." He holds his hand up, as if to prove it. I can see Finlay is impressed by the chunky gold rings that adorn most of his fingers.

"When were you there?" Finlay is quite the interviewer.

The President taps his nose. "It was when I was a Prospect," he says in a mysterious tone. Then he eyes Finlay appreciatively. He seems to have taken a shine to him. "You could be a Prospect," he says. "He could be the next Prospect, couldn't he, twinny?"

"I'm sure he would qualify admirably," says the Godfather, with a courteous nod toward Finlay.

The President gestures to the pointless Goth chain dangling from Finlay's trouser pocket. "That's good, that is. That's good Prospect gear."

What is he talking about? I'm sure Finlay doesn't know either, but he's not going to let on. Instead, he changes the subject. "So which country are you the president of?"

The President belches and wipes some sweet-and-sour sauce off his trousers. He doesn't look like a candidate for government to me, but I don't say so.

"It's not a country, see, it's a society," he replies. He eyes Finlay again and announces, "You'll need a Harley-Davidson if you're going to be a Prospect."

Finlay's face clears. "What, a motorbike? Are you talking about the Hells Angels?"

"He's always talking about the Hells Angels," says Lorraine in her flat voice.

So that's what he's the president of! Or does he just think he is?

The Godfather offers 'round some more rice. "I believe that boiling destroys ninety-nine percent of known germs," he tells us.

"Got any Buckies in there?" says the President to Ronnie.

By now there is a collection of empty cans and bottles at Ronnie's feet. Silently, he produces two green bottles with yellow labels from one of his bags. He hands one to the President and begins drinking the other himself. I'm not sure what it is, but the air is growing fumier by the minute. The President slurps away, appearing to have forgotten all about motorbikes and Prospects.

The room falls quiet. But something is stirring in my mind. Something troubling.

What was it Mary said about Ronnie that day in the park? "Ronnie'd do a runner if they gave him Unaccompanied"— that was it. At the time I couldn't make sense of it, but now I know what she meant: If they let Ronnie have time out from the hospital ward without a nurse to keep an eye on him, he would run away, get drunk, and not come back.

Why is Ronnie here now? Is he really better? Has he been discharged from hospital, like the Godfather? Or has he "done a runner"?

And what happens when someone does a runner? Does

the hospital get the police to track them down? Supposing the police come here and find me? Suddenly I don't feel like eating anymore.

The dog can tell that my appetite has gone. Sensing his advantage, he puts his paws on my lap and snuffles at my plate.

"Down, Zigger," commands the President.

Zigger ignores him. He snatches a chicken wing and retreats with it into a corner where he growls menacingly.

"That dog of yours is getting too much for me, Ronnie. I've had him for three weeks now. You'll have to take him back," says the President.

"They'll no' let Ronnie keep a dog on the ward," says Lorraine. "They willnae even let a dog visit the ward."

"Aye, but Ronnie's no' going back to the ward, are you, Ronnie? Ronnie's done a runner!"

So I'm right. I feel the panic rising in my chest. They'll come after him; I know they will. They'll find him, and they'll find me.

"Well, he's no' staying wi' me this time," says the President. "It's been bad enough having the dog, but I'm no' having the pair of them."

"Ronnie's no trouble," says Lorraine. All the same, I notice that she doesn't offer to put him up.

Ronnie himself doesn't join in this conversation about his future. But he puts down his bottle and looks sad.

"They can stay here!" says Mary.

My heart sinks.

To my relief, Finlay comes to my rescue. "But, Mary, what if the police come? We don't want them to find Leo."

There is a murmur of agreement from all Mary's friends. She hasn't told them exactly who I am, but as soon as the word *police* is mentioned, they are automatically on my side.

The President softens slightly. "It's Ronnie or the dog," he says. "One or the other. I'm no' having both of you."

"You have Ronnie, we'll have the dog, won't we, Leo, hen?" says Mary.

"But what about Midget?" I ask.

"They'll be pals, Midget and Zigger! They just need to get to know each other. It's just like wi' you and Sherlock."

I feel like telling Mary she's too kindhearted, but I can't keep bossing her about. And anyway, if she wasn't so kindhearted I wouldn't be here myself.

Ronnie seems happy with the arrangement. He smiles and hands 'round some cans. I shake my head, but Finlay takes one.

"Finlay! You're only just thirteen," I say.

"So what? You're not my mum."

"No, but I bet she wouldn't want you to. I bet she doesn't even know where you are."

"So? Stop preaching at me. It's not like your auntie and uncle know where *you* are." Finlay takes a defiant swig of his beer, then winces and splutters.

"I was building houses when I was twelve," says the President with a yawn.

What on earth has that got to do with anything? It's probably not true anyway.

Suddenly I'm fed up with the lot of them. Fed up with the smoky room and the smell of drink. I wish I could walk out of this crazy new world I'm living in, out into the cold clean night air. But of course I can't. I'm trapped.

Mary must have caught the look on my face. "What's the matter, hen? Do you no' like our Chinky?" She is eyeing the half-eaten food on my plate.

"I'm just not very hungry." I don't add that I hate the glutinous bright red stuff you get from Chinese takeaways. Dad sometimes used to cook for us—proper home cooking, and it didn't look or taste a bit like this.

As if Mary can read my thoughts, she says, "You'll have to cook the next banquet yourself."

"I can only do a few things," I say. "I could try to make my dad's special village dumplings—but I don't know where I'd get the ingredients."

"There's a Chinese supermarket in town," says Lorraine. She has perked up a bit, though the President is now asleep and snoring beside her.

"A Chinese supermarket! Let's go there after school tomorrow," says Finlay. He's trying to make it up with me after getting so stroppy about the drink.

It is a tempting idea. "But suppose I get spotted?"

"They'll all be Chinkies there—you'll blend in," says Mary.

"But on the way there, I mean?"

"I bet everyone's forgotten about you," says Finlay. "There hasn't been anything in the papers for over two weeks. I know—I'll lend you my school sweatshirt." He adds, unnecessarily, "I never wear it anyway," as he fiddles proudly with the zip of his Breakneck hoodie.

I'm beginning to feel a bit better. Perhaps I really can start going out again—and not just at the crack of dawn to do my drawings.

Mary's bell rings. The good feeling drains away.

"Hide, Ronnie!" whispers Lorraine.

Mary opens the bedroom door. "You too, Leo, hen."

Oh, no, I don't want to be cooped up in the wardrobe again, not with Ronnie.

The dog is quicker off the mark than either of us. He races into the bedroom.

Midget yowls, the dog barks, and a voice from outside shouts, "Open up!"

"It's no' the polis—it's Squirrel!" says the President.

And now everyone is laughing and gathering 'round the newcomer, who is a young man with a stack of papers. He has prominent front teeth and a red ponytail. It's not hard to see why they call him Squirrel.

"Hiya, Squirrel!" says Mary. "Meet my wee pals. This is Leo—she's a hideaway, like Ronnie. And Sherlock here's a paperboy, same as you!"

"You don't work for Rab, do you?" asks Finlay.

"No, I sell the *Big Issue*. It's 'cos I'm homeless. Well, I live in a hostel."

"You've no' sold many today," says Lorraine, picking a copy up and flicking through it.

"No." Squirrel looks despondent. "It's the rain. Everyone was in a rush."

"I'm no' in a rush! I'll buy one!" says Mary. Then I see her smile widen and her eyes brighten in the way I've come to recognize—the way that means she's going to say something over the top.

"I'll buy them all!" she says. "Aye, I'll buy the lot of them."

I'm about to try to stop her, when Lorraine says, "Look at this!" She turns her open paper 'round to show us.

There's a big picture of me.

"What does it say?" I grab another paper from the pile. While I'm finding the page, Lorraine starts to read aloud in a halting voice.

"MISSING—LEONORA WATTS-CHAN. Leonora left her aunt and uncle's house in Bristol on September 10 this year and has not made any contact with them since then. They supposed at first that she was in London, where she used to live before her parents were tragically killed in a plane crash, but now it is believed that she may be hiding somewhere in Glasgow."

The sick feeling comes back, worse than ever.

How do they know I'm in Glasgow?

I look at Mary. Her eyes are aglitter with the drama of it all. Then I look at Finlay. He looks like Macbeth in the banqueting scene. Guilty.

FINLAY ▪ ▪ ▪
In the Doghouse

Friday after school was Finlay's favorite time of the week and Rab's worst one. It was when the paperboys got paid.

Only one period left to get through now. Miss Cottrell was handing the English essays back.

"Yours was very good, Finlay," she said, sounding a little surprised. "'Specially the last paragraph about Macbeth's guilty conscience. Maybe you'd like to read Macbeth in the next scene. Ailsa, Laura, and Siobhan, you can be the three witches."

Finlay felt himself flushing, but he picked up his book.

"How now, you secret, black, and midnight hags," he began. That was quite a good description of Laura and Siobhan, actually, with their black clothes, long hair, and white Goth makeup, though not of Ailsa, with her regulation sweatshirt and neat chestnut curls.

Sweatshirt! That reminded him. He'd forgotten to bring his own sweatshirt in for Leo. It was supposed to be her disguise for going to Chinatown with him after school.

After the lesson, he hung back, hoping someone might have left a sweatshirt in the English room, but nobody had. He was surprised to see that Ailsa had lingered too; she seemed to be making heavy weather of packing away her books.

"Erm, Ailsa. . . ." Could he pluck up courage?

She looked up as if surprised to see him.

"You were good in that scene."

"Oh, thanks. So were you."

"Can I borrow your sweatshirt?" he blurted out.

Ailsa laughed. "What for? I didn't think you were into school uniform. I thought it was all Goth gear and crazy music."

"It's for this friend. . . . She really needs it, but I promised not to tell anyone why."

"Well, don't lose it." Ailsa took the sweatshirt off, hardly ruffling her curls. "Did you know Ross McGovern has asked me to be in his band?" she said.

"*You?*"

"Yes—don't look like that. I do play the drums, you know. Ross said you might be going to join it too?"

"Yeah, but I've got to get myself an electric guitar first. Thanks for the sweatshirt anyway." Finlay thrust it into his bag and went on his way. Ailsa was quite decent, really, and he felt mean having bad-mouthed her to Leo— another addition to his burden of guilt.

•   •   •

At the paper depot, Rab was handing out the meager wages as if his slaves were diddling him out of a fortune.

He eyed the skull on Finlay's school bag and said, "Where's the crossbones then?" before grudgingly taking three grubby fivers out of the till.

"Hey, I'm supposed to get £17.50 this week. I did Glennie Avenue again on Monday, remember?"

Rab muttered something about dropping someone's *Sun* in a puddle but then reluctantly put the extra coins into Finlay's palm. "Now you can afford some nail varnish remover," he said, with the nearest to a chuckle that he could manage.

Finlay ignored him manfully and set off along the canal toward Struan Drive. There was loud country-and-Western music coming from Mary's flat. It was her favorite Johnny Cash song, "I Walk the Line." He rang the bell, and immediately the music was drowned by loud barking.

No one answered straightaway. Finlay waited, and soon enough he heard the familiar crowing laughter from behind the spy hole.

"It's no' the polis, it's Sherlock!" Mary called out as she opened the door.

"Is that the Prospect?" came the President's slurred voice from the sitting room, speaking over the Johnny Cash song, which was still blaring out.

Zigger the dog rushed up to Finlay, placed his paws on his chest, and licked his face.

"You can come out, Leo, hen! It's only our Sherlock," shrieked Mary.

Leo emerged from the bedroom into the smoky hallway. She didn't look especially relieved.

"It's you again," she said rather coldly.

"Are you coming, then?"

"Coming where?"

"Remember, we're going to buy that Chinese food."

"You're joking—how can I now?"

"But I've got you that sweatshirt. You'll be fine."

"Oh, yes, I'll be fine now that everyone knows I'm in Glasgow." She glared at him, and he couldn't think what to say.

Mary burst into song. "I walk the line, and she'll be fine," she sang, changing the words of the Johnny Cash song as she danced around the tiny hallway. She took Zigger's paws off Finlay's chest so that the dog became her dancing partner.

"Because she's fine, we walk the line." The two of them disappeared into the sitting room.

Leo lowered her voice. "She's been like this all day. I'm sick of that music. And now the President and Lorraine have come 'round. They're boozing away, and it's so smoky! I hate it. I'm going to go mad trapped in here."

"Then come with me."

"No, I can't. I've got to lie low, haven't I? Thanks to you," she added bitterly.

"I'm sorry. I did ring that Missing People number, but it was before—"

"Yeah, I know, I know. Anyway, you'd better go."

Finlay hated being dismissed like this. "Well, if you make me a shopping list for your village dumplings, I'll go on my own," he said.

Mary was dancing back into the hall with Zigger. "Aye, Sherlock can shop!" she said.

"Not without any money, he can't."

This put a stop to the dance. Finlay understood: Mary's benefit money must have all been spent on biscuits and banquets.

"It's okay—I'll pay," he said recklessly.

Mary started singing again, fitting her words to the new song that was now playing.

"Sherlock's gonnae pay! Sherlock's gonnae pay! And I'll let that lonesome whistle blow my blues away."

"Well?" said Finlay to Leo. He half hoped she would say "don't be silly." His generous but hasty offer had pushed the electric guitar back to an even more distant horizon.

But, "All right, then," said Leo. "Do you know where the shop is?"

At the sound of the word *shop*, Zigger barked and started to wag his tail. He wriggled free from Mary's ballroom hold and raced into the sitting room.

"He thinks *shop* means 'walk,'" said Mary with one of the cackles that were beginning to get on Finlay's nerves.

Sure enough, Zigger came running back with his lead in his mouth.

"Hey, Prospect! Get us a six-pack and some Buckies!" called out the President.

"He can't. He's underage," snapped Leo. She shoved the shopping list into one of Finlay's hands and the end of the lead into the other.

TALKING TO THE BIRDS
3

There—it wasn't for long, was it? Daddy's back home now. Caitlin's been changing your water, hasn't she? She's been giving you lots of nice seeds. Caitlin's a good girl. We didn't tell Mummy, did we? We didn't tell Flo. Flo's a silly girl, she's got a silly little friend. I was only talking to her. You like it when I talk to you, don't you? Say Clemmy! Say Clever Clemmy! It was the child lock. I was going to unlock it. She was a silly little girl anyway. Who likes their swing? You do, don't you? See Saw Marjorie Daw. Don't be sad— Daddy's back now. He's got a clue. He's going to find her before they do. She's not silly. She's not like Flo's silly little friend. She knows I was only looking.

SHOPPING LIST FOR VILLAGE DUMPLINGS ▪ ▪ ▪

Bok choi (leafy kind)
Garlic
Sesame oil
½ cake tofu
Dim sum wrappers
Soy sauce
Ginger
5-spice powder
Spring onions
Prawns

FINLAY ▪ ▪ ▪
Chinatown

Finlay felt hard done by as he walked—or was rather dragged—toward the bus stop. He had heard of dogs walking their owners, but this was taking things to extremes: Zigger pulled so hard on the lead that you'd think his collar would have strangled him by now.

But it wasn't the dog that had put Finlay in his bad mood. It was Leo. It wasn't fair of her to blame him for telling the Missing People lot that he'd seen her in Glasgow. That was before he'd met her properly; it was when she was just the doughnut thief. Anyone would do the same—especially when there might be a reward.

And that wasn't the only thing. What really made Finlay's blood boil was the way Leo treated him like a ten-year-old kid brother. Like yesterday, when the President and those others were at Mary's drinking and smoking. Leo acted as if Finlay would instantly become an alcoholic just through having a few swigs of beer.

I'll show her, thought Finlay. Yes, he'd show her that he wasn't just a little kid who couldn't get anything right.

But maybe that was true. The only thing he *had* got right seemed to be alerting the world to the fact that Leo was in Glasgow. No, that wasn't all: He had tracked her down too, hadn't he? He *was* a good detective, just like Mary said. Well, now he would prove it to Leo too. He would track down her gran and granddad for her. That would wipe the haughty big-sister look off her face. He would make a start now!

But how? Leo had a list of all the Glasgow Chans, and Finlay wondered about going back and getting it. No, better to keep it a surprise. Where had she got that list anyway? It must be photocopied from the phone directory.

The library was just across the road from the bus stop. They had phone books in there and a photocopier. "Quick thinking, Sherlock," Finlay said to himself. (He secretly liked Mary's nickname for him.)

"That's not a guide dog, is it?" said the librarian. For a split second Finlay considered pretending to be blind, but his life was already quite complicated enough without that. He tied an indignant Zigger to the hook outside the swing door of the library.

When he came back out with the photocopied page of Chans, the dog was straining and barking furiously at a little girl in a lilac hooded top. The girl was clutching her mother and refusing to walk past Zigger and enter the building.

"Sorry, I think he thinks you're a burglar," said Finlay. He untied the dog and pulled him away.

Zigger was surprisingly docile on the bus—at first anyway. He sat at Finlay's feet, and when a woman sat down next to them and patted the dog's silky head, Finlay felt a pride akin to ownership.

Now was a chance to look at the Chan list. No less than three of them were in Geddes Street, which Finlay was sure was very near the Chinese supermarket. He should be able to check out numbers 6, 42, and 59, and still have time to do the shopping.

The woman got off, and a man in a knitted hat sat down in her place. Immediately, Zigger started to growl and bare his teeth.

"Watch it," said the man, edging away.

"He's just trying to make friends," said Finlay

unconvincingly. The bus was slowing down, and he added, "We're getting off here anyway, aren't we, Zigger?" though it wasn't in fact his stop.

He cursed not just Leo but Mary as he walked along Sauchiehall Street, with Zigger zigzagging ahead on the taut lead. "Fancy making me take you out—you're as crazy as her and her friends." His fingers were beginning to feel raw from having to grip the lead so hard. And every now and then, Zigger did his growling-and-teeth-baring act at some innocent-looking passerby. What made him single them out?

Finlay was having second thoughts about the Chan quest. Maybe that would be best for another day. But here was Geddes Street, and it did lead directly to the Chinese supermarket. And here was number 59, and yes, one of the buzzers had a label saying "Chan" beside it! Supposing he got it right first go? Statistically Leo's grandparents might just as well live here as at any of the other addresses. That would change the look on her face, wouldn't it? Finlay rang the bell. He tried to imagine Leo's face lit up by astonishment and admiration, and failed.

There was no answer.

Number 42 didn't come to the door either, but while Finlay waited, a Chinese woman approached the house, key in hand.

"Excuse me, are you Mrs. Chan . . . or Miss Chan . . . ?"

"No, Chan top floor. Flat 3/2. But not in."

The woman was about to let herself in. Finlay seized his chance. "Do you know them, the Chans?" he asked.

"Yes, I know them. Mrs. Chan my sister. If you want, I can give message."

"Thank you. Er . . . have they lived here a long time?"

"My sister husband come in 1970. Come from Hong Kong."

"And do they have any children?"

"No, no children. What is message, please?"

"Oh, that's all right. There's no message. I think it's the wrong family."

"That is no problem," said the woman, looking unperturbed, as if Chan seekers came every day to the house. She let herself in.

Finlay was disappointed, but at least that was one Chan he could cross out.

Zigger pulled him relentlessly along Geddes Street. Outside number 6, a couple of boys were sitting on the low wall drinking Cokes and eating crisps. One of them looked Chinese and was fiddling with a baseball cap.

With the briefest of warning growls, Zigger rushed up and seized the cap in his jaws.

"Bad dog!" said Finlay. He tried to tug the cap from Zigger's mouth, but the dog just growled and clung on for dear life. Luckily, the boys started laughing.

"I'm sorry," said Finlay.

"It's cool," said one boy. The other one said, "Watch this," and held out a crisp for Zigger.

Faced with the choice between cap and crisp, an expression of terrible indecision came over the dog's face, but when the boy made to withdraw the crisp Zigger hastily dropped the cap and snatched it. The boys laughed again; Finlay too.

"Cool dog," said the first boy, who was now sitting safely on his cap. "How old is he?"

"I don't know—he's not mine," said Finlay. "I'm just taking him for a walk."

"Do you live 'round here?" The boy didn't have a Chinese accent, but he didn't sound Scottish either.

"No," said Finlay. "No, I'm just looking for someone, someone called Chan."

The boy grinned. "That's me!" he said. "Or was it my mum or dad you wanted?"

"No, I don't think so. I'm looking for some older people."

"What, my granddad, you mean? He's not here yet— not till next month. He's still in Manchester."

Of course. That was the accent. It made Finlay think of *Coronation Street*, his mum's favorite television program.

"So is that where you're from?"

"Yeah, we just moved here six months ago."

Another cross on the list then.

"Who are these old folks you're looking for anyway?" asked the Chinese boy.

"Oh, they're . . . my grandparents."

The boy seemed surprised. "You don't look very Chinese."

"No." Finlay was stumped, but only for a second. "No, it's funny, isn't it? I take after my mum. She's Scottish. My dad left us when I was a baby, and I'm trying to track down his mum and dad."

"Wouldn't they still be at their old house? Like, where your dad lived when he was a kid?"

"But I don't know where that is."

"You don't know much, do you?"

"I do know that my dad used to go to the music college."

"You should ask there, then," said the other boy, who had been too busy feeding crisps to Zigger to join in the conversation. "It's just down the road."

"Good idea. Thanks," said Finlay.

But first there was the shopping to do.

The Chinese supermarket was in a sunken area by a motorway flyover. Finlay tied Zigger up outside, noticing that there was a pets' hospital opposite. "Be good or you might end up in there," he told him.

He took Leo's scrawled shopping list out of his pocket and couldn't help thinking of the witches' cauldron in *Macbeth*. There were no eyes of newt or toes of frog on the list, but a lot of the things sounded almost as weird: bok choi, tofu, dim sum. What were they all?

Bok choi was clearly some kind of vegetable. There were various strange-looking ones to choose from. One kind was very long and thin and white; another kind looked a bit like a hedgehog. But Leo had written "leafy kind" in brackets. Finlay found a heap of green leaves in a box. He picked one up and nibbled it; it had a slightly unpleasant bitter taste.

"Is Asian pennywort," said a small elderly man, appearing beside Finlay. "Good for bladder. Make into tea. Bladder will be very strong. Also liver. Use just a little."

That didn't sound right. In the end the man pointed out the bok choi, which looked a bit like spinach but with thick white stalks. But there were two slightly different kinds. Which was the right one, and how much to get? "One from north, one from south," said the man, which wasn't much help either. Finlay took a handful of each and hoped for the best.

What about the next item on the list: half a cake of tofu? Finlay found a fridge full of white cheesy-looking stuff in different-sized packets. The shopkeeper confirmed that this was indeed tofu but looked blank when asked which one was a "cake." Finlay played safe and chose a large block.

It took a long time, searching among the shelves of seaweed and sauces, to find the other ingredients, and when he asked for prawns, the shopkeeper pointed him out of the building, saying, "Fishmonger. 'Round corner."

There were two kinds of prawns—dead pink ones and crawling-about gray ones. Finlay had a sneaky feeling that the crawling-about kind were the ones he should get, but he couldn't bring himself to buy them. They'd probably start crawling all over the bus.

That is, if there was enough money left for the bus. What with buying two alternatives for some of the things, Finlay was horrified to find that the whole lot came to nearly all his wages.

"We might have to walk home, Zigger," he said as he rejoined the dog outside the shop. Zigger barked and wagged his tail at the sound of his favorite word. A scrawny woman was standing nearby, observing them with folded arms. Why did she look so disapproving?

And then Finlay smelled it—not a Chinese smell this time; just plain disgusting dog poo, coming from the sole of his foot.

"Zigger! You bad dog!" Finlay scolded, as he did his best to wipe his foot on the edge of the curb.

The woman said nothing but pointed to a notice outside the pets' hospital. Finlay screwed up his eyes and could just make out the words: "Poop scoops available within."

Intimidated, he crossed the road and followed the signs to the entrance. Inside, a receptionist handed him a pack containing a cardboard shovel and a bag labeled "Woopsi-bag" with a picture of a guilty-looking dog on it.

Nearly retching and still under the scrawny woman's scrutiny, Finlay scooped up the poo and deposited it into the woopsi-bag.

"You're a nightmare dog," he scolded Zigger, though maybe *nightmare* wasn't quite the right word; the whole outing felt more like one of those endless tiring dreams where you have an impossible task to complete and everything goes wrong.

The onlooker was still looking on. She seemed to be better at pointing than speaking. This time she indicated a bin attached to a nearby lamppost. Finlay dumped the smelly bag into it, congratulating himself on not throwing away the bok choi or the tofu by mistake, which he would have done in one of those dreams. But turning around, he found that Zigger had discovered the prawns and was helping himself to a whiskery mouthful.

At that moment, Finlay wished he'd never met Leo. He wished he was at home, with a cup of tea and a plate of toast.

"But we're not going to give up now," he told the unrepentant Zigger as he untied him, turned his back on the scrawny woman, and headed toward the music college.

The wonderful smell of fresh coffee wafted down the stairs into the modern entrance hall with its walls of pale orange bricks. There must be a café up there. Too bad there was no money left. Hoping that his foot didn't still smell of poo, Finlay went up to the inquiry desk. A man in uniform was reading a newspaper.

"Excuse me, I'm doing a school project about musicians,"

he lied. "I need to find out about where one of your old students used to live. But maybe your records don't go back that far. This would be about twenty years ago."

"Twenty years—that's nothing," said the man. "Our records go back to the 1950s. Earlier in some cases." He spoke proudly, as if he personally had written every student's name and address into an ancient volume.

"Oh, good. Well, this guy was called something Chan. I don't know the exact dates he was here, but he played the flute and—"

"Just a minute, sonny. I didn't say we could divulge any information about anyone."

"But I thought—"

"It doesn't matter what you thought. It's the Data Protection Act, see. We can't divulge any information about anyone."

"But this man's dead now. It's not like I'm going to stalk him or anything." The man looked unimpressed, so Finlay changed tack. "In any case, it's not him, it's his parents I'm trying to track down. And they weren't students here, were they? You don't need to protect them, surely?"

"That's not the point. The point is the Data Protection Act. It's against the law to—"

"To divulge any information about anyone?"

"Aye." The man looked put out to have his favorite words taken away from him.

"Oh." Finlay was unwilling to accept defeat so easily. He

thought about his mum, who had an embarrassing habit of complaining in shops. What would *she* say next?

"Can I speak to the manager?" Finlay asked.

The man laughed. "You don't give up, do you?" he said. "If you mean the Records Officer, she's off today. But she'd just tell you the same thing. It's all to do with the—"

"Data Protection Act?"

"Aye." The miffed expression again.

"Well, thanks anyway." Finlay turned to go. He oughtn't to leave the disastrous dog outside for any longer.

But the man relented and called after him, "There's one thing you could do."

"What's that?"

"You could write a letter care of us, and we could forward it."

"I see." Finlay toyed with this idea. He'd have to ask Leo first, and maybe she'd think it was too risky. . . .

"That's what I told the other guy."

"What other guy?"

"The other guy who came asking about this Chan student. Was it your teacher, maybe? No, I think he said he was some kind of relation. He didn't look Chinese, mind."

"What did he look like?"

"I can't say—except for the glasses. Very thick glasses, he had, those magnifying ones. And some sort of hat—aye, a flat hat."

"I see," said Finlay. In his normal cheeky mood he might have said, "I thought you weren't supposed to divulge any information about anyone." But he didn't, because he suddenly felt cold.

UNCLE JOHN'S LETTER ▪ ▪ ▪

Flat 1b, 19 Pusely Place, Bristol

Mr. and Mrs. Chan
c/o The Royal Scottish Academy of Music
    and Drama
100 Renfrew Street
Glasgow G2 3DB

October 5

Dear Mr. and Mrs. Chan,
Although we have never met, I am a relation by marriage of your family.

Your son, Matthew Chan, was the partner—or common-law husband—of Harriet Watts. Miss Watts's sister Sarah is my wife.

I do not know if you are aware of the tragic death in an air crash of your son and Miss Watts, when they were on their way home from an orchestra tour in Spain three months ago. My wife and I extend our heartfelt sympathy to you both. We would have notified you at the time, but we had no address for you, and it was only recently that we thought of contacting you via the music school that your son attended.

We understand that all contact between yourselves and your son was severed as a result of his relationship with Miss Watts and are therefore unaware whether you know of the existence of their daughter, Leonora, who is now fifteen.

Following the death of her parents, Leonora was entrusted to the care of my wife and myself, being the closest known relatives. Unfortunately, our niece, despite every effort on our part to ensure her comfort, and despite appearing to enjoy the company of her cousins (our two daughters, Florence and Caitlin), disappeared from our home on September 10 of this year and has not been seen since. We have reason to suspect that Leonora may have traveled to Glasgow, perhaps with the intention of seeking you out, and we are appealing to you for news of her.

Our niece was understandably in a disturbed frame of mind following the death of her parents, and it is possible she may not fully have appreciated our good intentions. Indeed, that she may even have circulated some untruths about the care she received in our home. Should this be the case, we would appeal to your better judgment and request that for her welfare you write with the utmost urgency to the above address (and NOT to our previous Bristol address, which Leonora may have given you). A good home and school await my niece.

Yours sincerely,

John Baldwin

MIDNIGHT MARY

Leo!
Leo, hen!
Wakey wakey!
Rise and shine!
Rise and shine and walk the line!

Leo, hen, wake up!
It's time for the dancing!

Aye, it's the middle of the night.
The middle of the night when the stars
    shine bright.

It's time for the banquet!
It's time for the bash.
You and me and Johnny Cash.
Cash, cash, lots of cash.

Where is it?

Where's the cash?

Someone's hidden it.

It's under the pillows. It's under the sofa.

Get up, hen! They've hidden the cash.

They've hidden the money for the
banquet.

It's no' there. They've taken it.

That Lorraine, she's taken it.

That big-mouth, that long-tongue liar.

Liar, liar, long-tongue liar,

Tell the lads her tongue's on fire.

No, I didnae spend it.

No, I'll no' go to sleep.

We're celebrating!

Jammie Dodgers—that's what we need.

Cornflakes—that's what we need.

Where's that salad bowl?

We're making cornflake salad.

Dumplings—that's what we need.

Leo, hen, make some more of they
dumplings.

They dumplings were fit for a king.

Macbeth! We'll feed Macbeth. We'll feed
the king of Scotland.

No, I'll no' turn it down.

Turn up Johnny! Turn up the cash! Turn
up the cushions.

Tell 'em that God's gonna cut 'em down.

Tell 'em that God's gonna cut 'em down.

Dance, hen. Dance, Leo, hen!

If ye'll no' dance, I'll dance with Zigger.

He's a beauty, he's a barker, he's a barker in
the park.

Hark, hark, the dogs do bark.

The beggars are coming to town.

We'll no' be beggars, we'll be rich, we'll be
rolling,

We'll be on the payroll. You and me and
the Godfather.

Look in the mirror, what do you see?

One two three, I see me!

Turn it 'round, it's unlucky. Turn it to the
wall.

Help me, hen! Help me, Leo, hen!

Tell 'em that God's gonna cut 'em down.

Tell 'em that God's gonna cut 'em down.

Footsteps

I don't care if someone does recognize me. I had to get out. I had to.

So now I've got a new job and a new name.

The job is Ross McGovern's paper round. Ross wasn't very good at getting up in the mornings, so Rab sacked him and Finlay introduced me. Or, rather, he introduced Emma Clark—that's what we told Rab I was called.

I've got a disguise too. Not just the school sweatshirt, but some white makeup. It's the Goth look, though I think I look more like a ghost. Rab thinks so too. "Does that head come off? Can you tuck it under your arm?" he asked me. That's about the only question he *did* ask, thank goodness.

Glennie Avenue has old-fashioned paving stones. Don't tread on the cracks and you'll be all right. Tread on the cracks, and a dragon will get you. I'm not a child anymore, and I don't believe in dragons, but I do avoid the cracks—just in case.

It's all right. No one will recognize me. No one is after me. Everyone has forgotten about me. I haven't been in the papers since that *Big Issue* piece nearly two weeks ago.

Oh, it's so good to be outside, away from the clutter and the smoke and the noise. And away from *her*.

Poor Mary. She's such a kind soul, and I owe such a lot to

her. She's funny too, and plucky. But now she's got this wild look in her eyes all the time. And she just talks nonsense, streams and streams of it. And worst of all, she doesn't sleep.

At least the others aren't 'round so much, those friends of hers, if you can call them friends. Ronnie's back in hospital, and I haven't seen Squirrel or the President since the night I cooked the dumplings. I don't think it was the dumplings that put them off (though the President was a bit rude about them—he said they were like something you'd find hiding under a rock). No, it must be because Mary's benefit has run out that they've drifted away. The Godfather has dropped in once or twice, and Lorraine did come over the other day, but Mary wouldn't let her in. She seems to think Lorraine is plotting against her.

That's it—147 Glennie Avenue, the last house. It's eight forty-five. Finlay and the others will be on their way to school, but I'll have to go back to Mary's now. Please let her be asleep!

I'll go back along the canal. It looks different from when I sketched it a month ago. I'd like to sketch it again, with all those leaves floating in it.

This is the place where I snatched Finlay's camera. Funny to think he was the enemy then. Now I don't know what I'd do without him. He's got me this job, and this disguise. Yes, he's better at running my life than his own. But I do worry about him. He spends so much time at Mary's, and he keeps missing bits of school.

Finlay doesn't seem to care. And he doesn't give up. He still thinks he can track down my grandparents. He wants me to write a letter for the music college to forward to them. I'm still dithering about that. It seems so risky: Supposing someone at the college opened it? But wouldn't that be better than just vegetating in Mary's flat doing nothing?

All these questions flitting 'round my head. What am I going to do about Finlay? What am I going to do about Mary? What am I going to do about me?

It's so quiet here by the canal. Except for a bird singing in that tree, and the leaves crunching under my feet. Now the bird's stopped. If I stop, there'll be silence. Lovely, lovely silence.

But there's not. I can still hear a crunching of leaves. Someone's walking along behind me.

Don't be so jumpy. Just set off again. Don't run and don't look 'round. Just walk normally, but don't tread on the cracks. If you don't tread on the cracks, it will be all right; it will only be someone going to work or to the shops. If you tread on a crack, it could be him.

"Hey, you!"

A man's voice. He doesn't sound Scottish.

"I want to talk to you." *His* voice? Finlay thinks he's here, in Glasgow, looking for me.

Walk faster, but don't run.

"Wait a minute!" He's walking faster too. He's running.

I'm running too. Run, run—but not on the cracks.

Through the gap in the hedge. 'Round the corner, into Endred Close. There's a parked car in a driveway. I duck down behind it.

He's turned the corner. Let him walk on past!

He doesn't.

"What do you think you're doing?"

I'm cornered. He's blocking the driveway. I look up.

It's not him. Of course it's not. It's a man with a newspaper, and he's pointing to the front page.

I must be in the paper again. How could I have missed it?

"It's not me! I just look like her," I tell the man, trying to keep the panic out of my voice.

"Don't talk rubbish. I saw you put it through the letter box," he says. "Don't you people ever get the message?"

"What message?"

"I'm not taking the *Herald* anymore. I've left two messages on the answer phone, and I spoke to the boy last week, but you still keep delivering it. Here, take it." He thrusts the paper into my hand. "And tell that Rab of yours I don't want to see it on my bill."

TALKING TO THE BIRDS
4

Look at this! What is it? It's a lantern, look! Can Georgie make it swing? Clever boy! Georgie Porgy, pudding and pie, kissed the girls and made them cry. I didn't kiss the girls. I wasn't following her. I was going that way anyway. Who's got a nice soft neck then? Who's got a nice soft chest then? We're still waiting. We're waiting for that letter. Are you waiting too? Don't worry, Daddy's going to open the door. That's right, out you come. Have a fly around. It's nice to fly around, isn't it, Georgie? Don't worry, they're not going to lock Daddy up.

FINLAY
The Spy

It was a rainy Saturday morning. The Barras market was emptier than usual as Finlay splashed through the puddles between the food stalls, breathing in the aromas of Bill's Burgers and Mr. Chung's Spicy Chicken Wings. He'd woken late and missed breakfast, but there was no time to stop and buy anything—and no money, come to that.

Marina was waiting for him in the doughnut van.

"Sorry I'm late. The bus got held up," Finlay told her.

"I've heard that one before. You watch out or I'll be giving you one of they enemas, or whatever you call them."

"N of Ms," said Finlay. "Don't remind me—I've had three this week."

"What for? Not more forgery, I hope."

"No. One was for failure to come equipped with adequate classroom materials, one was for persistent garrulousness, and the other was . . . oh, yes, persistent inattention."

"They like long words, don't they? So what's with the persistent inattention then, Finlay? I've been noticing a spot of that myself recently. Is it something on your mind?"

"No, not really. Well, sort of . . ."

Marina's blue eyes had that piercing look, as if they could drill their way through to Finlay's innermost secrets, and for a moment he was tempted to blurt out everything. How he'd spent most of his savings on those dumpling ingredients; how he was worried that thanks to him Leo's uncle was on her trail; how Ailsa Coutts kept on at him because he still hadn't given her back her sweatshirt.

Then there was all the trouble with his parents. Why were they so suspicious all the time? They seemed to be part of some parental spy ring; Finlay had even found a file on his dad's computer labeled "Finlay's Friends." That must be how they got Ross McGovern's number and found out from Ross's parents that he hadn't been there the night he'd come back from Mary's smelling of alcohol. How could he go on seeing Leo and taking Zigger for walks with them breathing down his neck?

Finlay was saved from replying by a couple of girls who bought a bag of doughnuts to share, and after that Marina lost interest in his problems. "Five doughnuts for a pound," she called out, leaning out of the van and waving a bag about rather halfheartedly. A few more potential customers were drifting past, with anoraks and umbrellas, but Marina seemed less interested in them than in the huddle around the new hot-dog van opposite.

"Why do they all want that muck?" she grumbled.

"They're tasty," said Finlay, who was still hungry.

"We'll have to think about going savory, Finlay. We'll have to start a new line. What do you think—beef burgers? Chicken wings?"

"There's stalls for those already. How about roast pigeons?" said Finlay with a sly look. He knew that Marina's husband kept racing pigeons.

"You let my Kenny hear that and it'll be roast schoolboys. Tell you what, son. You go and do a spot of market research."

"What's that?"

"I thought they'd tell you at school, with all their long, posh words. It's finding out what the punters want."

"You mean what things are popular."

"Aye, and if there's any glaring gaps. I can spare you for a quarter of an hour or so."

"Can I taste anything?"

Marina rolled her eyes. "I might have guessed that was coming. Here you are." She handed him the pound coin the two girls had given her. Finlay put it in the pocket of his baggy jeans.

"What's happened to that chain of yours? The one you usually have dangling out of your pocket?"

"I swapped it with Ross McGovern for a T-shirt."

"Going off the Goth look, are we?"

"No, I just liked the T-shirt," said Finlay, though actually Marina was right. Somehow the spiky accessories and the black clothes were beginning to lose their attraction. So were the Goth girls in his class; Ailsa Coutts was actually a lot prettier than they were, without the dark lipstick or ghostly cheeks. And when Finlay had given Leo the white makeup and black nail varnish for her papergirl disguise, he couldn't help thinking how silly it looked on her and wondering for the first time if he looked silly to other people.

"Off you go, then," said Marina. "Spy out the land."

This was a job after Finlay's heart, and one which he was sure he could do well, thanks to his newly developed detective skills. His confidence was only slightly dented when Marina called out after him, "Your trousers are falling down!" She obviously didn't realize that this was an intentional part of his new look. Along with the chain, Finlay had abandoned his usual spiky belt.

He retraced his steps, this time inspecting the different food stalls keenly. Mr. Chung's Spicy Chicken Wings was clearly doing better than Bill's Burgers. Finlay considered investing in some chicken wings; that way he could get into conversation with Mr. Chung and ask him if he knew any Chans—a detective's work is never done. But the chicken wings cost two pounds a portion. Carlito's Chips with Curry Sauce were much better value at 80p, but as he approached the stall, he heard a burst of laughter from a neighboring van and decided to investigate.

A boy who didn't look much older than Finlay was standing outside the van handing out flyers. Finlay took one. DIM SUMPTUOUS!!! it said in giant capitals, with some Chinese writing beneath, and under that, "Authentic dim sum. Genuine Chinese family food like in China, freshly steamed on the premises."

Inside the van, a girl of about eighteen was taking the lid off a bamboo basket. "You taste these, you'll never go to your local takeaway again," she said to two cheery-looking men, one tall and the other short.

"You'd talk the hind legs off a donkey, you would," said the tall man.

"That's probably what she puts in these!" said the short one, and they both roared with laughter. The Chinese girl, who was transferring the contents of the basket into two plastic containers with a pair of tongs, joined in the laughter. "There's a money-back guarantee if you find any donkey's legs in here," she said. "It's all good stuff. It's my granny's secret recipe. Very nutritious. It'll make you grow," she said to the short man, who guffawed again. "Do you have another recipe to make my pal shrink?" he asked.

The man in need of shrinking noticed Finlay's interest. "Are you queuing up to take your life in your hands?" he asked.

"Aye, he can be our taster," said his friend. "Just like the Roman emperors had. Here, lad, check this out, just in case it's poisoned!" He held out the plastic box to Finlay. Inside were six dumplings looking very like the ones Leo had made.

"I've had these before. My friend makes them," said Finlay.

"But not in Glasgow, I don't think," said the girl. "Not the same as this."

Finlay popped one of the dumplings in his mouth. It tasted just like Leo's ones, except that the dough was a slightly different texture, more moist and stretchy. "I think my friend uses dough from a packet—these are better," he said.

"Does this advertising come free, or is he on the payroll?" the tall man asked the girl. His companion roared appreciatively and added, "At least he's not dropped dead—that's the main thing."

Still laughing, the two men picked up their food boxes and departed.

Finlay's neck was tingling with excitement.

"Why did you think my friend's dumplings wouldn't taste like this?" he asked the girl.

"Well, dim sum is a special kind of cooking. Not many people do it in their homes—usually it's just in restaurants. And there's not many dim sum restaurants in Glasgow. My grandparents used to own one, but it closed down. I don't think another restaurant would do this flavor—it's a special recipe from my granny's village."

Village dumplings. Wasn't that what Leo had called her ones? The tingling spread down Finlay's back.

"Would you mind telling me your name?"

"I'm Jacqueline."

"No, I mean your surname."

The girl laughed. "Why do you want to know my surname? Ah, I know, you want to look me up in the telephone book! But I haven't got time for a boyfriend, you know! And I think you're a bit young for me. Sorry! Anyway, my surname is Yeung."

"Oh." This wasn't the name Finlay had expected to hear. Suddenly he felt flat, and foolish.

"Never mind. You're a nice boy. I'm sure you'll find a good woman."

"Hang on—what about your grandparents? Did they have a different name from you?"

"My *grandparents*! My granny would definitely be too old for you. You're such a funny boy! But I like nosy boys. Yes, my mum's mum and dad do have a different surname. But why do you want to know?"

"Please just tell me—I'll explain afterward."

"All right. It's not a secret anyway. They're called Mr. and Mrs. Mo."

That sick, disappointed feeling again.

"Okay. Well, sorry to bother you. The dumpling things are really good anyway." Finlay turned to go.

"No, don't go yet, you nosy boy. It's my turn to ask some questions."

"Well. . . ." Finlay wasn't keen on this idea. "I can't stay long."

"What's *your* name?"

"It's Finlay. Anyway, I must go."

"Wait a minute. What about your cook friend? Is he Chinese?"

"It's not a he, it's a she," said Finlay and then regretted it. Still, he hadn't really given anything away. "Look, I've got to get back to the doughnut van."

"The doughnut van? So you're a rival! Maybe a spy! Andy, I've caught a spy!"

The boy who was handing out the flyers turned and grinned. He looked friendly, and Jacqueline was just teasing, but Finlay still felt uncomfortable.

"See you, then," he said gruffly, and turned back through

the rain. He'd been away for longer than his allotted quarter of an hour, and he hadn't even spent Marina's pound.

"Well then?" Marina asked him. "What's it to be?"

"Sorry?"

"Our new savory line."

"Oh, yes. Maybe chips," mumbled Finlay. "But not with curry sauce—someone's doing that already."

"Aye, we don't want to end up knifed by a rival gang," said Marina. "Maybe chip butties. Or how about deep-fried pizza?"

"Yes, could be good." Finlay turned his back and busied himself stirring the doughnut mixture. He wasn't feeling chatty. He'd been so sure when he tasted that dumpling that he was on the right trail, especially when Jacqueline had said that they were quite a rarity in Glasgow. But he'd just been jumping to conclusions, like his math teacher said he always did. He was a failure at mathematics, a failure as a detective, a failure as a friend.

The next couple of hours passed slowly, with only a few doughnut and candy floss sales. Marina continued to gaze morosely at the thriving hot-dog van, and Finlay brooded about dumplings and Chans.

Toward noon there was a flurry of customers. "Get with it, Finlay. The sugar tray's empty," Marina scolded him as she scooped out some more doughnuts from the hot oil.

"Sorry." Finlay shook some sugar out of the canister and rolled the doughnuts in it, then put five of them in a bag. "That's a pound," he said, turning around to the customer.

"You see—I've tracked you down. I'm a spy too!" It was the girl from the dumpling stall.

"Oh, it's you" was all Finlay could find to say.

"Aren't you going to introduce me to your pal, Finlay?" asked Marina.

"This is Jacqueline Yeung, and this is Marina," said Finlay awkwardly.

"Are you at Finlay's school?" Marina asked Jacqueline.

"No, no, I've only just met him. He's a nice boy—isn't he?—but so nosy! No, I'm at the art school. I'm nearly nineteen. I just look like a tiny kid," said Jacqueline. "No one ever lets me into clubs or pubs unless I have my passport with me. It makes me sick. Anyway, Finlay, you were going to tell me about your Chinese cook friend. Is she Chinese?"

"Who's that then, Finlay? I never knew you'd been hobnobbing with Chinese cooks."

Talk about being nosy! The pair of them were more than Finlay could take.

"She's just someone I vaguely know," he said.

"And why were you so interested in my grandparents? Did you think they might be relations of your friend or something?"

Jacqueline was a bit too bright for Finlay's liking.

Fortunately, Marina was now serving another customer, so Finlay didn't have to worry about her overhearing. Maybe honesty was the best policy. He lowered his voice and said, "Yes. My friend's grandparents run a restaurant too, or they used to do. But their name is Chan."

"Chan! Well, maybe they are related, then. That's my great-uncle's name—my granny's brother. He was the one who started the restaurant, back in the sixties."

"Do you know if he had a son?"

"Yes, he did. But he doesn't like to talk about him. There was some family feud or something, and the son moved away." Jacqueline obviously noticed the excitement in Finlay's face. "Why, does that fit in with your friend's story? So maybe she's related to me! A cousin or something! What's her name? Does she go to your school?"

"Er. . . ." Finlay had promised Leo he wouldn't disclose her name or whereabouts to anyone.

Marina had finished serving the customer. "Tongue-tied, are we, Finlay? That's not like you. What's happened to that persistent garrulousness of yours?"

But Jacqueline sensed that Finlay didn't want to talk in front of Marina. "Have you still got that flyer? Our number's on it. Give us a ring, or get your friend to." And she was off.

"What's with you and all these Chinese lassies?" asked Marina. "Remember that one you were chasing after? The one that took the doughnuts? And now this one seems to be chasing after *you*! And what about this Chinese chef—who's she? Finlay? There you go again, persistent inattention."

Finlay said nothing, but his smile was the happiest one Marina had ever seen on his face.

CHAN JING'S LETTER

64 Burn Street
Glasgow

October 21

Dear Mr. Baldwin,

Thank you for your letter. A social worker from the Glasgow Center for the Chinese Elderly is helping me to write this reply, as I am not very good at writing or reading English.

You are right that my son, Matthew, stopped being my son when he chose to live together with the English woman you mention in your letter. I did not know they had a child. This child has not been to my house.

yours sincerely,
Chan Jing

"Hello, Kim Yeung speaking."

"Oh, hi. Um, is Jacqueline there?"

"No, she's at the art school. I'm her mum. Who's speaking, please?"

"I'm . . . well, I'm a friend of Finlay's. He met Jacqueline at the Barras."

> *SHE'S A DEVIL WOMAN.*
>
> *GONNA BURN, GONNA BURN MY SOUL.*

"Sorry, I can't hear you very well. That music is very loud."

"Yes, sorry. Mary, can you turn it down?"

"We can't turn down the dancing! Only the devil turns down the dancing!"

"Could you tell me when Jacqueline will be in?"

"Sometime after four. Shall I give her a message?"

> *I THOUGHT I WAS IN HEAVEN*
>
> *TILL I LOOKED INTO HER EYES.*
>
> *FOUND MY ANGEL WOMAN*
>
> *WAS A DEVIL IN DISGUISE.*

"Well, maybe you could say Finlay's friend called."

"I know who you are now! You're the girl Jacqueline has been telling me about. She's never stopped talking about you. She thinks you're a cousin or something."

"Well, I don't know. I've been trying to—"

I TOOK MY FATHER'S RIFLE,
SHOT HER AND SHE FELL.
THEN I KNEW MY DEVIL WOMAN
HAD DRAGGED ME DOWN TO HELL.

"Listen, why don't we give Jacqueline a surprise? Why don't you come 'round tomorrow? Come to 61 Burn Street."

"Well, it's a bit hard for me to . . . all right, yes! Yes, thank you very much. What time shall I come?"

"Don't go, Leo! She's at it! She's devilish! Your woman's devilish!"

"Come around six. You can eat with us."

"Are you sure?"

"Of course. And you can bring that wee boy, if you like. Our Jacqueline keeps talking about him too."

"Thank you very much. That's so kind of you. I'll ask him."

"Don't ask Sherlock. Sherlock mustnae meet the devil. She's in with that Lorraine—they're in it together. They're at it!"

"Sorry?"

"It's okay, that was just my friend Mary."

"Is everything all right?"

"Yes, everything's fine. I'll see you tomorrow at six."

DEVIL WOMAN
GONNA BURN, GONNA BURN MY SOUL.

Burn Street

Here it is—number 61 Burn Street. A red sandstone house, the second to last in a row of no-nonsense tenement buildings.

There are no front gardens, but at the end of the road is a small grassy square. Through the railings I can see a dog lifting its leg against a tree.

"Look, Finlay, it's a sycamore!"

"It looks more like an Alsatian to me."

"Not the dog, the tree, silly!"

"So what? This isn't a nature ramble."

"Didn't I tell you? Dad said their house was near a big sycamore tree. Finlay, I think this is the right place!"

Finlay rings the bell. I feel shaky, just like when I was changing in the station loo—that fear of the unknown.

"I'll buzz you up," comes a voice.

A door on the first landing is opened by a pretty Chinese girl with her hair in a ponytail. Her eyes light on Finlay. "It's *you*! My little spy. I should have guessed! Mum's been playing one of her tricks on me—she said it was . . . oh, never mind. What a nice surprise anyway! Come in."

Inside the little hallway, she turns to me. "Sorry, I'm Jacqueline. I'm always gabbling away and forgetting to tell people the basic things. And you're Finlay's cook friend, but I haven't even asked you your name."

Before I have time to answer, an older, plumper version of Jacqueline appears and says, "Welcome, Finlay! Welcome, Finlay's friend!"

I hesitate a second. I'm so used to hiding my real name that I nearly say, "I'm Emma." But if these people are really my relations, it's time to drop the paper-round disguise. "I'm Leonora," I say, "but everyone calls me Leo for short."

The name doesn't seem to ring a bell with her. She replies, "And I'm Kim, Jacqueline's mum."

"My trick-playing mum. She said you were going to be some boring old people from the community center."

"Not a trick—a surprise." Kim looks pleased with herself. "Like I always say, surprise is the spice of the dumplings of life."

"Mum, don't start up on the Chinese proverbs. In any case, Leo knows all there is to know about dumplings already, so I've heard."

"No, I don't," I start to protest, but it's difficult to get a word in edgeways with these two.

"I am being so rude, not offering you tea straightaway. I will go and make some. Jacqueline, you introduce our guests."

Kim disappears through one door off the hallway, and Jacqueline opens another. "The clan is in here," she says. "Well, most of them. Gran is in the kitchen, and Dad works late on Tuesdays."

Two boys and a girl are sitting in front of a large television.

They get up as we come in and grin shyly. The girl looks about twelve, and the boys are maybe fourteen and sixteen.

I feel shy too. So many new people, and I didn't even know they existed. How are they related to me? And what about my grandparents—where are they?

"Andy and Finlay, you met at the Barras, didn't you? This is Leo, everyone—she's a kind of cousin, but I expect she'll tell us all about that. Oh, and this is Suzanne, and this is Jonathan. Of course that's just their English names. We've all got Chinese names too. I suppose you must have a Chinese name as well, Leo?"

"My Chinese name is nearly the same as my English one—it's Liu, but no one ever calls me that. Well, my dad used to. . . ."

They're all looking at me expectantly, but I can't bring myself to talk about Dad just now. How silly, when that's why I'm here.

"Cool pictures," says Finlay. Feeling grateful to him, I turn and look at the wall behind the sofa.

"Those are Jacqueline's masterpieces," says the boy called Andy.

There are three of them, and they are more like banners or painted silk shawls than straightforward pictures. The middle one shows a very long airplane with a face at every window. The two at each side are tall rather than long; the left-hand one is of a green hill covered in people and cows; on the right is a red house overhung by a tree with a bird perched on it and a fish and bell dangling from two of its branches.

"They're lovely. Do they tell a story?"

"Yes." Jacqueline looks pleased to be asked, but Andy groans. "Oh, no, now we're going to get the running commentary."

"It's my mum's story, really," says Jacqueline. "Maybe she'll tell you later."

And here is Kim, with a lacquered tray of tiny, dainty teacups. She turns off the television and pours out tea from a china pot with a bamboo handle. It's Chinese tea, like Dad used to make, pale greenish yellow, with no milk or sugar. Finlay winces as he sips his. The younger boy, Jonathan, notices. "We've got some Irn-Bru if you'd rather," he says, and now he and Finlay are drinking the disgusting fizzy stuff from orange-colored cans and talking about hip-hop. The ice is beginning to break.

Jacqueline is perched beside me on the arm of the sofa. "So, Leo, Finlay seems to think you're a twig on our family tree. How come we've never known about you? Have you always lived in Glasgow? You don't sound Scottish."

"How do you know what the poor girl sounds like?" says Andy. "You ask her all these questions, but you never give her a chance to open her mouth."

"It's okay," I say. Embarrassingly, I can feel tears pricking my eyes. I've waited so long to meet these people, and now I should be getting down to the nitty-gritty of working out who they are and how they're related to me. But I just feel so overwhelmed.

Jacqueline must see the budding tears. She pats my arm. "Sorry, Leo, I forgot—you really want to hear Mum's story, don't you?"

"I think there is a lot of storytelling to be done," says Kim. "But remember the proverb: 'The one who talks too much will have to eat cold food.'"

Jacqueline rolls her eyes. "Why don't you just lead us to the hot food, then, Mum, instead of talking in ancient Chinese proverbs?"

"I'm afraid we don't have a separate dining room," Kim apologizes, as we follow her across the hallway toward some wonderful smells.

Inside the large kitchen/dining room, an elderly lady is bowing and smiling. My heart gives a sudden jump—can this be her? Granny, Grandma, whatever I'm supposed to call her?

But, "This is my mother," says Kim. "I think she is maybe a kind of aunt for you. You can call her Auntie Luli."

The old lady smiles again and gestures toward a table in an alcove.

A sumptuous spread of food is laid out. In the center is a whole chicken, complete with beak and claws. Actually, it's not really a whole chicken. When you look closely, you can see it's been chopped into pieces and then reassembled.

"Leo, you sit next to Suzanne, then you can do some

eating, not just talking," says Kim. Suzanne smiles shyly as she sits down beside me. On my other side is Finlay, and next to him sits Jacqueline.

Around the chicken are six or seven dishes of food, and every place has its own little bowl of rice and pair of chopsticks.

"Maybe you would like a knife and fork?" suggests Suzanne in a whispery voice.

"No, I'm used to chopsticks," I say.

"Please help yourselves," says Kim.

I can see that Finlay is scanning the table for something familiar-looking.

"If it moves, eat it!" says Jacqueline with a laugh. When Finlay tries unsuccessfully to laugh along, she pats his arm and says, "I'm only teasing you. There are no sea slugs or beetles here! I'll tell you what everything is." She rattles off the names of the dishes, but I only take in a few of them: tofu with pickled cabbage, shredded pork with Chinese radish, and steamed eggs with dried scallops.

This definitely beats Mary's banquet; it looks more like the food Dad used to cook, but there's so much of it! And Auntie Luli keeps bringing more dishes: a salad of lotus roots, some pieces of spicy lamb on the bone.

If only I felt hungrier! If only my ridiculous nerves would stop gnawing at my stomach!

The chicken disappears quite quickly, but now an enormous boiled fish has replaced it as the centerpiece.

"Have an eye, Finlay!" says Jacqueline. "They're the best part—they'll make you such a clever boy at school." She laughs when he looks horrified. Instead, she gouges out one of the fish eyes and passes it to Auntie Luli, who is at last sitting down with us.

The old lady pops it in her mouth, then smiles and points to her own eyes. "Good for see," she says.

"My mother doesn't speak much English—sorry," Kim says. She says something in Chinese to the old lady, who shakes her head and replies.

"I was asking if she had made any dumplings—but she said no, because she is scared they would not be good enough for you. Jacqueline has told us all that you are a great dumpling chef, Leo."

"I'm not!" I protest. "I just used to help Dad sometimes. They were his favorite food, ever since he was a little boy." And now it feels easier to talk about home, I don't know why. "Dad always called them village dumplings. They were the kind his mum and dad used to have in their village before they came to Scotland."

Kim is nodding, and I find myself telling all I know about Dad's childhood, which isn't much. I don't get up to the plane crash, but I tell them how he met Mum and quarreled with his parents.

Again, Kim translates for Auntie Luli. She nods vigorously. Then she puts her hands up to one side of her face and waggles her fingers. She is miming someone playing the flute!

"Yes, I have heard this story before," says Kim. "And Jacqueline told me your grandparents were called Chan."

"Like me, yes."

"Well, it's a very common name, of course. But I think it would be too much coincidence to have two stories like that. I think that your grandfather is Auntie Luli's brother."

"What, Uncle Jing, you mean?" says Jonathan.

"Is he . . . is he still alive?" I ask.

"Yes, he is. Actually, he still lives in the old house—it's just across the road. But he spends most of his time in the center for the elderly. They have lots of activities there, even Tai Chi and Ping-Pong. In the evenings, he's at home, but he just likes being by himself. He doesn't like going out or having visitors—even us."

"And his wife—my grandmother?"

Kim shakes her head sadly. "I'm afraid she died four years ago."

"Oh."

Why do I feel so sad about someone I've never met?

"Of course, we didn't have your father's address, to tell him."

"No, of course not."

I don't just feel sad, I feel angry, angry with Dad. Why did he never tell me properly about his mother? Why did he never make up with her? And now it's too late, for all of us.

A tear drops into my rice bowl, then another one. I wipe my eyes furiously, but more tears form.

"Sorry," I say. "Could I just go to the toilet?"

When I come out, Jacqueline and Kim are in the sitting room. Jacqueline pats a place beside her on the sofa and puts a protective arm around me. "The boys are listening to music, and Suzanne's doing her homework," she says. "Would you like to hear Mum's story now, Leo, or would it all just be too much?"

"No, please, I'd like to hear it," I say.

KIM'S STORY

KIM: I was fifteen when I came to Britain—the same age as you, Leo. It was autumn, and the leaves were falling off the trees. Even now, every autumn when I see those falling leaves, I think of that time.

What a different life! We came from the countryside where we knew everyone into a big city with lots of people, and all of them speaking a foreign language.

LEO: Had you learnt any English at school?

KIM: Only things like *A* is for *Apple, B* is for *Book.* And on many days I didn't go to school. If Mum was ill, I had to do the farm work instead. Well, maybe farm is not the right word. It was really just a small field, just like every family had, for growing rice and vegetables.

JACQUELINE: And the cow, Mum! Tell her about the cow!

KIM: Jacqueline is so keen on that cow! Everyone had a cow, which lived in the house and was set free each day to eat the grass on the hill. After school the children would go out and fetch the cows. We all had sticks to wave about and guide the cows, or for hitting their bums if they stood still, but mostly I didn't need to use my stick. Our cow was happy to come home with me. But one time I couldn't find her. I looked and I looked and I called and I called, but she didn't come. I felt like crying, but I tried not to, because people would just laugh at me and think I was weak. When it was nearly dark, I decided I would have to go back down and tell my mum. I was nearly home when I heard a mooing sound. I looked 'round and saw that she was following me. My mum said she had just got lost, but I had a feeling that the cow wanted to give me a surprise.

JACQUELINE: Maybe that's how you learnt to play tricks, Mum.

KIM: Not tricks—surprises!

LEO: Now I understand the first picture, Jacqueline. That hill is the one behind your mum's house, isn't it?

JACQUELINE: Yes, and the children are all leading the

cows home. All except one. Can you see the girl without the cow?

LEO: Yes, there she is—she's got a stick but no cow. And there's the cow, hiding behind that tree!

JACQUELINE: Well spotted!

LEO: There aren't any men in the picture—it's all women and children.

KIM: That's what it was like. There were hardly any men in the village, just a few old ones who sat outside their houses.

LEO: Where were the young ones, then?

KIM: All away in western countries. My father went to Britain when I was just a baby.

LEO: By himself?

KIM: Yes. Most of the men went on their own to start off with, without the family. The plan was to get work and start saving, until they had made enough money for the family to come over and join them. They would send money back home—some of them did anyway. Others forgot about their home, but my dad wasn't like that.

LEO: So didn't you ever see him?

KIM: Only every four years, when he came back for a visit. That's how I got two younger brothers! I remember the first time he came back. He was just this strange man to me, and I was upset and angry because he slept in my mother's bed. I used to sleep there and cuddle her every night, but when Dad came back, he told me to go to the other bedroom and sleep on my own. I was glad when it was time for him to go back to Britain.

LEO: What did he do there?

KIM: He worked in a restaurant—well, lots of restaurants, mainly as a chef. He kept moving around till he got quite a good job helping to run a takeaway restaurant in Leeds. He used to send us letters, and we would collect them from the village shop. Then one day he wrote and said it was time for us all to join him. He sent us the money for our plane tickets.

LEO: Now I understand the second picture. It's the aeroplane you came on, isn't it?

KIM: Yes, and one of those faces at the windows is me, isn't it, Jacqueline?

JACQUELINE: Yes, that one in the middle.

LEO: The one with closed eyes?

JACQUELINE: Yes. I painted Mum like that because she told me she kept dropping asleep on the journey.

KIM: That's true. I had no idea it would be so long. Every time I woke up I asked my mum, "Are we nearly there yet?" but it seemed to last forever.

LEO: So many windows, and so many faces.

KIM: My dad came to meet us at Heathrow. He knew we wouldn't have a clue how to change planes.

LEO: I suppose he was really good at English by then?

KIM: No, he wasn't. Actually, he could hardly speak it at all.

LEO: What, after fifteen years?

KIM: Well, you see, he only really mixed with other Chinese people. He was a chef, so he was hidden away in a kitchen, not meeting the customers. And he had to work long shifts, and different ones each week, so it would have been hard for him to go to evening classes, even if he had wanted to. But he did very well. He saved up enough money to buy a flat above the takeaway shop. At first we stayed inside that flat all day long. My mum was too shy to go out, and because of his job Dad brought us all the food we needed, so we didn't have to do much shopping.

LEO: Didn't you go to school?

KIM: Not for a week or even longer, but then this English lady from the flat upstairs came and knocked at the door. She was a nice lady but very bossy. She took my brothers off to the local primary school and me to the secondary. The head teacher wasn't too keen to have me—he said it would be hard to teach someone who didn't speak English—but the lady just said, "That's your problem, Headmaster," and she left me there. It was awful. I just sat in the classroom, and I couldn't understand a word. In the playground, it was even worse. At the end of the day, the lady came back to collect me. She saw how unhappy I was, and she said she was very sorry. After that she found out about an English language teaching center, and I went there for two years.

LEO: Did you learn quite quickly?

KIM: Not as quickly as my brothers! I found it hard to

understand what people were saying. For a little while I had a job in a restaurant. I was a waitress, but I couldn't understand the customers. All the words sounded the same. One time I brought someone a glass of milk when he had asked for the bill. After that they moved me to the kitchen to wash up, but when my father heard that he was angry because he said I wouldn't learn any English. He was very keen for me to learn English, even though he could hardly speak it himself. He made me leave that job, and after that I worked part-time in his takeaway shop.

LEO: Did you get on with your father?

KIM: So-so. Not so much at first, because he never let me do anything. He always said I was too young and made me come home at nine o'clock. That made me cross because in Hong Kong I'd had a lot of responsibilities—I was more like an adult. I was a good girl, and I didn't want to run wild or anything. It was funny, really, because Dad didn't realize that the real danger was under his nose.

LEO: How do you mean?

KIM: I got very friendly with his partner in the shop—a man called Tony Yeung. Tony was eight years older than me, and I don't think Dad thought he could be a possible boyfriend. But we used to chat behind the counter, flirting really, and sometimes after the shop closed, I would sneak out and meet him when my parents were playing a game of mah-jongg. Those games went on for ages sometimes.

JACQUELINE: You never told me that before, Mum. I can't believe you were so sneaky! And when I think what you and Dad were like when I was fifteen! Breathing down my neck all the time.

KIM: All parents are the same. You'll be just like that when you're a parent—wait and see. Anyway, I was seventeen by this time, and we weren't just fooling around. By the time my parents found out, we had decided to get engaged.

LEO: What did they say about that?

KIM: Actually, they were okay about it. They liked Tony. We got married when I was nineteen, and soon afterward all of us moved to Glasgow. That's where Jacqueline and the others were born.

LEO: And that's the third picture, isn't it? That red house and the tree—is that the sycamore tree in the square?

JACQUELINE: Well, partly. But it's also the Glasgow tree—"the tree that never grew."

LEO: How do you mean?

JACQUELINE: It's part of the coat of arms of Saint Mungo, Glasgow's saint. Along with the bird that never flew, the fish that never swam, and the bell that never rang. They've all got legends about them.

KIM: But I don't think Leo needs to hear those legends just yet—she's looking a bit tired. I'm sorry, Leo. Has my story gone on too long for you?

LEO: No, not at all. And I'd love to hear the legends sometime, but what I really want to know is why you moved to Glasgow.

KIM: Ah. That's where your grandfather comes into the story. My uncle Jing. He was my mother's brother, and he came from the same village as us. He moved to the UK about four years after my father went there, and his wife went with him.

LEO: My grandmother.

KIM: Yes. They didn't have any children then. It was before your dad was born.

LEO: Did you meet them when you moved?

KIM: No. Not for a while. They were already in Glasgow, and of course it was quite a journey from Leeds. But soon after Tony and I got married, your grandparents opened a second restaurant in Glasgow, and they invited us up to help them run it. Our takeaway shop wasn't doing that well anymore—so many others had opened up—so we agreed to go.

LEO: And did you meet my father?

KIM: No, I never did. By that stage the quarrel had happened, and Uncle Jing and Auntie Mei didn't like to talk about him. I gathered he had gone off with some woman they disapproved of.

LEO: That was my mother.

KIM: I'm sorry, Leo. Am I upsetting you? It must be sad for you that your granny has died.

LEO: It's not just my granny.

What's the matter? We're all ruffled. We're all upset. Is it because Daddy's going away again? Don't worry. That lady from upstairs is going to give you your seeds. Daddy won't be gone for long. This is the last time. I know the address now. He says she's not there, but Daddy doesn't believe him. I'll find her. I'm going to find her before they find her. She won't say what they tell her; she'll say what I tell her. Yes, you're pretty. On you hop. You love your daddy, don't you?

FINLAY
Black and White

Finlay sat in his bedroom and opened his English file. He stared at the heading on the otherwise blank sheet of paper: "What does the sleepwalking scene reveal about Lady Macbeth's character?"

Leo would know; she was the expert on the Macbeth household and would be only too happy to pass on her expertise to Finlay. But if he went around to find her at Mary's, he would only have to lie to his mum about where he was going, and Finlay was sick of that. No, it was time for an evening in—a lie-free evening.

He tried to concentrate on reading through the scene.

They'd read it out in class that day, and Miss Cottrell had chosen Finlay to act the doctor who got called in by a serving maid because Lady Macbeth was wandering about the battlements in the middle of the night, washing her hands and coming out with all this dead giveaway stuff about the murders. Finlay found himself wondering if he ever talked in his sleep and, if so, whether he came out with anything revealing. Maybe that was how his parents were so good at spotting his deceptions.

"Finlay!" The door opened. Why couldn't Mum ever knock? And why did she have that unnaturally sweet smile on her face? "What was that film called—the one you saw last night with Ross?"

"I already told you, *Black and White*. Look, Mum, I've got to do my homework."

"What was it about?"

"It was . . . er, about a penguin with superpowers. I don't know why Ross was so keen to see it. It was rubbish."

"I think it sounds good. What sort of superpowers did this penguin have?"

"You know, like . . . well, stopping global warming and things."

"That sounds interesting. How did he do that?"

"He kind of flapped his flippers and . . . well, it was a bit complicated—I can't really describe it. Anyway, Mum, I can't talk now. I'm trying to write this essay."

"You don't know, do you? You didn't even see the film."

"We did! Well, we saw the beginning, but like I said, it was rubbish, so we went and got a Chinese takeaway instead."

"That's strange, because according to his mother, Ross didn't go out last night."

"Mum! You've been spying on me again!"

"And what am I supposed to do when you won't ever tell me the truth?"

"I'm thirteen. I'm not a baby. I can't tell you every little thing."

"That doesn't mean you have to tell me a pack of lies."

"They're not really lies. . . . Anyway, what do you expect when you're always interrogating me and trying to catch me out? You're like the Spanish Inquisition, you and Dad."

"Finlay, are you hiding something?"

"There you go again. Just lay off!"

"Listen, Finlay, we're worried about you. And so is the school. At that parents' evening, at least three of the teachers said you were having difficulty concentrating."

"Well, you're the one who's stopping me concentrating now. Just let me get on with my homework!"

"Can't you see that we care about you?"

"You *don't* care about me. You just want to meddle into everything and give me a bad name with all my friends."

"Just tell me, Finlay. Tell me where you were last night. Tell me the truth for once."

"I *did* have a Chinese meal."

"I said the truth."

"See! You don't believe me when I *do* tell the truth. You're always like that! You always think the worst of me!" Finlay jumped up and dodged past Mum, who was standing in the doorway.

"Where are you going?"

"I'm going to see a Chinese girl and a mad old lady," shouted Finlay. "But of course you won't believe me!" And he slammed the front door behind him.

LEO
The Meeting

The last time I was in a café, it was the middle of the night. Now it's the middle of the day. I felt jittery then, and if anything I feel even more jittery now.

The art school eatery is very different from Midnight Oil with its baths and mirrors. Loud music with a growly bass washes over the students who are playing pool, eating macaroni and cheese off paper plates, or drinking at the bar. It's quite dark, which is reassuring, and I'm sitting on a bench opposite Jacqueline, with my back to the wall so no one can sneak up on me. All the same, it feels so public! I can't help trying to hide behind the plasticated menu.

Jacqueline laughs. "Talk about drawing attention to yourself!" she says. "Remember, you're with me—I'm a kind of camouflage; no one's going to be looking for *two* Chinese girls. So stop looking like an escaped convict!"

I try to laugh too. "Well, I feel like one. I've been cooped up for nearly six weeks—till last night, that is."

"Haven't you been out at all?"

"Only to do my paper round, but it's not properly light then. Oh, and I did used to get up early and sketch by the canal. But I gave that up after I was in the *Big Issue*."

"You never told me about that!"

"What, the *Big Issue*?"

"No, the sketching."

"Well, I've only known you for a day—less than a day!"

"It's funny isn't it? I feel we've known each other for ages. So you're an artist like me? A budding Picasso?"

"Not really. I just do these pastel sketches. Actually, I've brought my sketchbook to show you." I take it out of my faithful hold-all.

"Great!" Jacqueline wipes her hands on her paper napkin and then opens the book. Suddenly I feel shy.

"I can tell who this is," she says. She's looking at the one of Dad playing the flute. "And this must be your mum."

"Yes. Her hair didn't really look like that. She used to wear it loose, but I'd been plaiting it just for fun."

Jacqueline reaches across the table and squeezes my hand. She doesn't say any more about those pictures, but flicks through till she reaches the Glasgow ones.

Then, "What a fat cat!" she says.

"That's Midget, Mary's cat. And that next one is the bridge over the canal near her house."

Jacqueline turns the page. "I really like the reflections of those clouds and berries."

"That was when I was sitting on the bridge."

She studies one of the pictures for longer. "Is this one *your* reflection?"

"It was going to be, but then Finlay appeared and gave me a fright. I never finished that picture."

"Finlay!" Jacqueline laughs. "I really like that boy. He's so funny—clever too." She turns another page. "Hey, here he is!"

"Yes, I did that one at Mary's."

"What a scowl! And look at that devil pendant."

"That was when he was really into being a Goth. I think that's wearing off a bit now."

"Who's this dog?"

"Zigger—he's one of Mary's waifs and strays, like me."

"What about Mary? I can't see any of her."

"That's because she never keeps still long enough. She doesn't even sleep."

"That must be tiring for you."

"Yes, it is." I take a sip of my coffee. I could say more. I could tell her how much I long to move out—but I don't. Nor do I admit that the main reason for tracking down my long-lost relations was the hope that they would give me a home. That seems impossible now. The Yeungs' flat isn't very big, and it's clearly bursting at the seams. And from what they've told me about my grandfather, it doesn't sound as if he welcomes visitors, let alone a live-in granddaughter.

"I'm quite nervous about meeting him," I say as Jacqueline hands me back the sketchbook.

"Who, Uncle Jing? Don't be. Your granddad can be a bit gruff, but he's more sociable when he's at the elderly center. But listen, we can always go there another day if you don't feel ready."

"No, let's go now. Let's stick to the plan."

Jacqueline grins, then squeezes my hand again. "I tell you what—would you like a quick look 'round the art school first? It's quite a famous building, actually. It was designed by this brilliant architect called Charles Rennie Mackintosh. They do guided tours, but I can whisk you 'round for free."

The art school is across the road from the café. Above two huge windows with curved iron brackets, an iron bird sits on top of a turret, like a weather vane.

"Look! It's like the one in your picture."

"Yes, it's one of the Glasgow signs."

"And I like those iron leaves and roses on the railings."

"If you like the outside, I bet you'll love the inside."

And I do. I've never been to school, and I always picture schools and colleges as dull institutional buildings with dozens of identical doors leading off dozens of identical corridors. But this building doesn't feel like an institution.

The walls are of dark wood, yet light is everywhere. It streams through windows and skylights. It glints on dainty pink and purple glass hearts embedded in hanging lamps and in squirly iron rafters.

Jacqueline takes me along a corridor lined with statues—a Madonna and child, a winged headless angel, a warrior with a serpent twining 'round his muscular legs. "They were put there for students to draw, but most students today aren't that interested—they're too busy making what they call personal statements. I'll show you." She opens a door into a room full of pictures. "This is the student exhibition gallery."

"I see what you mean. That one's a bit strange."

Someone has torn up a lot of holiday postcards and has glued the fragments on to a life-size photograph of a fridge, like fridge magnets. The picture is entitled *Wish You.*

Another one is of a massive scarlet scaffold with a jumble of cryptic symbols below it, as if two ancient Egyptian giants had been interrupted in a game of Hangman. It's hard to see why this one is called *Self-portrait.*

But I like three pictures of a path disappearing into a wood, overshadowed by trees, and then emerging from the wood and branching in two. And there's another one of a woman with wild hair and a sad moonlike face, which somehow makes me think of Mary in one of her rare quiet moments.

"It's all so exciting! I wish I could come here."

"Well, why shouldn't you? You could apply in a couple of years."

"But don't you need to have A-levels or Highers or something?"

"If they really like your work, then they only ask for Standard Grade Art and English."

I don't see how I could get those. Missing people can't sit exams.

Jacqueline is obviously a mind reader. "We'll find a way," she says. "But now I think we'd better go and see your granddad."

The Chinese elderly center is just 'round the corner from the art school, but it's a different world. The smell is the first thing that hits me—a foody smell, warm, salty, and spicy, familiar and somehow comforting. A smell can bring back so much. It brings back our kitchen at home, with Dad cooking noodles in black bean sauce, and Mum's cello practice floating through from the next room.

A smiling young man sits at the reception desk behind a china Buddha. He says something to Jacqueline in Chinese. She replies, then he glances at me, nods, and gestures toward the stairs. He's still smiling, but did I detect a flicker of something? Puzzlement, suspicion, even? No, I'm being paranoid again.

"Uncle Jing is in the common room upstairs," says Jacqueline. "Shall we go and see him?"

I nod and swallow.

"Did you say who I was?" I whisper as we round the bend in the stairs.

"No, I just said you were a friend."

The smell is fading, but now there are sounds: soft jabbering voices, and the irregular rhythm of a Ping-Pong ball. A door on the landing is open. Jacqueline smiles at me encouragingly, and we go in.

Four squat women look up from a card game and beam at us. Two agile men carry on with the Ping-Pong game. A few people are reading newspapers attached to bamboo sticks, and there is a cluster watching a Chinese television channel.

Which one is he?

Jacqueline looks 'round swiftly, then approaches one of the newspaper readers.

He looks up, and I see Dad's face.

Older, lined, but still Dad. And I was expecting a stranger.

He nods at Jacqueline and smiles vaguely. He looks the way Dad looked when he was interrupted in the middle of a detective story—as if he is still in another world.

Jacqueline speaks to him in Chinese. This is it. She's telling him. Her voice seems to halt and falter. Either she's not fluent in the language or it's difficult to say what she has to say.

He's not smiling anymore. He looks perplexed. His eyes dart to my face and then away. Jacqueline is looking at me; I sense that she is willing me to speak.

I say, "Hello, Grandfather."

He won't meet my eye. The perplexed expression has gone now. He just looks . . . blank. He's shaking his head. Now he's saying something, slowly, five or six words. He says them twice, I think.

Jacqueline turns to me again, as if she's about to speak, but she says nothing. I've never seen her at a loss for words like this.

I say the words for her. "He doesn't want to know me, does he?"

FINLAY
The Raveled Sleeve

Finlay had nearly reached Struan Drive when he remembered that Leo probably wouldn't be there. Hadn't she arranged to meet up with Jacqueline? Despite being the one who had united the two cousins, Finlay felt a stab of jealousy. Would Leo still have time for him now? It seemed unfair that the reward for his detective work should be to lose her to her new family.

He felt a little sour when he thought of Jacqueline. She had been so taken with him, in her teasing way, at the Barras, but she seemed to have transferred all her curiosity and chat to Leo.

But maybe he was just in a self-pitying mood because of the row with Mum. He tried telling himself that Jacqueline's younger brothers were good fun, and the quiet sister seemed nice too; perhaps he would be making friends rather than losing them.

"Sherlock!" Mary's shrill voice broke into Finlay's thoughts. There she was, outside the flats, with a thin ginger cat in her arms. He had seen the cat before; it belonged to someone on the ground floor, he thought. Mary was wearing a long leather coat that was much too big for her; the sleeves flopped down, hiding her hands, and Finlay wondered how she had managed to pick the cat up.

"Hi, Mary. Who've you got there?"

"It's Midget's long-lost twin. No, not a twin. There were four of them, four. Not twins, not triplets . . . quadrupeds!"

"Quadruplets, do you mean?"

"Aye! Quadruplets! Quadruplet quadrupeds! A squad of quads, sent by God!" Mary screeched with laughter, and the cat jumped down from her arms. Mary's expression changed from mirth to anguish. "No, no, no!" she cried. "Divided at birth, united in age!" She stooped in an attempt to grab the cat, but it ran into a bush.

Finlay had told Mum he was going to see a "mad old lady," but until now he hadn't really thought of Mary as mad—well, not properly mad, just a bit over the top. But seeing her out here wandering about in that strange coat, pursuing a cat, and talking a load of rubbish, he realized it was something more than that. Her eyes, always bright, had an extra gleam to them—maybe something like Lady Macbeth in the sleepwalking scene, he thought.

Finlay touched her shoulder. "I like your coat" was all he could think of to say.

"It's the Godfather's coat—the long-lost twin!" declared Mary. She seemed to have forgotten about the cat, and Finlay took the opportunity to steer her up to flat 2/1.

Zigger bounded to the door, but his welcome barks couldn't drown out the loud music. It was Johnny Cash, as usual, this time singing "Ring of Fire."

"Maybe we should turn that music down," said Finlay.

"Aye, turn it down! Turn down the music! Turn down the bed! Turn down the job application!" cried Mary, clapping her floppy sleeves together as she led the way into the sitting room.

Leo wasn't there, but Squirrel, the *Big Issue* seller, was sitting on the floor, drinking from a bottle of Irn-Bru and dipping into a monster-sized bag of crisps. On the sofa sprawled the President, with a cigarette in one hand, a can of lager in the other, and several empty cans at his feet. Beside him sat the Godfather with a large saucepan on his lap. The pan was full of chocolate Hob Nobs. Mary's benefit check must have come in.

"Certainly, certainly." The Godfather jumped to his feet and turned the volume on the CD player down. Then he held out a hand to Finlay. "Delighted to meet you again," he said. The other hand still held the saucepan. "Would you care for one?" he asked. "I am assured that they are unadulterated."

"Hiya, Prospect!" the President greeted Finlay. He tapped his nose and added, "I'm working on your initiation. . . . When are you going to gie twinny his coat back?" he asked Mary.

"It's the leader's coat," said Mary solemnly, unbuttoning it. She felt in a pocket and pulled out a red hat with a pom-pom on it. "I must give back the leader's crown too," she said. She threw the hat to the Godfather. It landed in the pan of biscuits.

"I am very much obliged," said the Godfather. He sat back down on the sofa, placed the pan on his lap, and pulled the hat onto his head.

The effect was dramatic. Zigger, who all this time had been begging for crisps from Squirrel, growled and made a rush for the Godfather. He seized the man's trouser leg and, still growling between clenched teeth, began to tug. The Godfather jumped to his feet amid a cascade of biscuits. "Away, hound! Away!" he cried, waggling his trapped leg. Meanwhile, his twin brother roared with laughter.

"Let the leader be! Set the leader free!" cried Mary.

"Down, Zigger! Bad boy!" scolded Finlay. Zigger took no notice.

"I think it's the hat," said Squirrel. "Try taking it off."

The Godfather removed the hat and instantly the dog loosened his grip.

"He's always been like that," said Squirrel. "He hates hats. He's Ronnie's dog, remember. The polis were always picking Ronnie up, right? I remember when Zigger was just a puppy and he went for one of the polis outside a pub."

That explained a lot of things, Finlay realized. He had thought that Zigger's occasional attacks on members of the public were random, like airport staff doing a body search on every fifth or tenth person, but now he could see a pattern. The girl outside the library with the hooded anorak, the man on the bus, the boy in the baseball cap—in each case it was the headgear that had alarmed and provoked the dog.

Zigger was now happily devouring a Hob Nob while the Godfather retrieved the rest. On the sofa, the President belched. "Any more Tennent's, Mary?" he asked in a slurred voice. "Our Prospect could do with a drop of liquid."

"Maybe I could have a cup of tea," said Finlay, surprising himself. Without Leo there to disapprove, he found he didn't really want to be part of the boozing, smoking, scrounging scene.

"Liquid for Sherlock! Liquid for Sherlock!" Mary flapped a leather sleeve at the two brothers on the sofa. "Up! Up! It's under the cushions! That Lorraine'll no' find it there. Up! Up and away!"

The Godfather got up readily. The President grumbled, "You're off your heid, Mary" (rather tactlessly, Finlay thought), but then dropped his last empty can and dislodged himself reluctantly. "Gie's the coat, then," he said. "We'll be off to Froggie's."

Mary slipped the coat off. Underneath it she was wearing a nylon nightdress, and she looked thinner than ever, Finlay thought; she'd been providing for all these friends but eating practically nothing herself. She knelt down and began to scrabble at the sofa cushions, not seeming to notice that two of her guests were departing. The third one, Squirrel, had fallen asleep on the floor.

"Thank you for the hospitality, Mary," said the Godfather, now reunited with his coat. He glanced warily at Zigger as he stuffed the red hat back into the pocket, then held out a hand to Finlay. "I hope we meet on some future occasion."

"Aye, see ya, Prospect," said the President. "I'll have to talk to you about that Harley-Davidson."

As the door closed behind them, Mary was still busy with the cushions. She was pulling them off the sofa and flinging them on the floor, all the time muttering incoherently about liquid and Lorraine. Then, "Here they are!" she cried, and burst into song:

"Ten black bottles, sitting on the wall. / Ten black bottles, sitting in the sofa!"

Finlay knelt beside her. Inside the sofa was a stash of at least twenty tiny bottles.

"Nail varnish!"

"They're yours, pal. They're your bounty."

Finlay picked up one of the bottles and looked at the

label. It was the Black Death shade he used to wear but had now gone off, along with the whole Goth look. "Thank you, Mary, that's really kind, but—"

"The best for the best," she said.

"But you shouldn't be spending your money on me. Mary, you're not eating properly. I really think—"

Mary ignored his protests. "All things go full circle," she said cryptically.

Why couldn't she talk sense? Finlay felt out of his depth. "What do you mean?" he asked.

"Stand in the middle!" Mary placed her hands on Finlay's shoulders and pushed him gently into the middle of the room. He stood there bewildered while she arranged the bottles in a circle around his feet. "It's your satellite!" she said.

"Look, Mary. . . ." Again, Finlay didn't know how to respond, and in any case, Mary wasn't listening. She was once more busying herself with the sofa cushions and rearranging them in an outer circle around the bottles.

"All things go full circle," she said again.

"How about that tea, Mary?" said Finlay, as if trying to break a spell. It seemed to work. "That's the brew for us!" cried Mary. "No' the Irn-Bru—the tea brew! The leafy leafy tea-leafy brew!"

"You sit down, and I'll make it." Finlay picked up a sofa cushion, hoping to restore the room to normality.

But, "No! I'll make the tea brew! I'll make the Hebrew tea brew!"

Finlay followed Mary into the kitchen. Instead of filling the kettle, she started twiddling the knobs of the gas cooker.

"What are you doing, Mary? We don't need the gas on."

All four gas rings had sprung to life and were blazing away.

"We need the rings of fire!" said Mary.

"No, we don't! It's an electric kettle." Finlay was trying hard to keep the conversation normal, though he knew very well that Mary wouldn't respond in a logical way.

Mary was staring in fascination at the flames as she raised and reduced the level of each ring in turn.

A panicky feeling was rising in Finlay's chest. What was it Mum always said? Three deep breaths. He took them as he stirred the three spoonfuls of sugar into Mary's tea. Then, thinking of Mum, he had an idea.

"I know! You could have a nice lie down. My mum sometimes has a cup of tea in bed in the afternoons. She says it's rejuvenating."

"Rejuvenation!" The idea, or perhaps just the word, appealed to Mary. "Rejuvenation and jubilation!" she chanted as she allowed Finlay to lead her toward the bedroom. His hope was that once in bed Mary would fall asleep. Sleep was surely what she needed most. There was something in *Macbeth* about that, Finlay remembered now—something about sleep "knitting up the raveled sleeve of care." Miss Cottrell had said that meant that sleep could untangle people's minds. If anyone's mind needed untangling, Mary's did.

But when he opened the bedroom door, the room was far from restful. The bedclothes were all on the floor mixed up with Leo's oil pastels, and the bare mattress was covered in strange multicolored marks, rather like Egyptian hieroglyphics. The only normal feature in the scene was the cat, Midget, who was curled up at the bottom of the bed, purring obliviously.

"Mary! What have you been doing?"

"I had to tell them. But the mattress was too heavy." Tears filled Mary's eyes.

"Tell who what?"

"About the leader." The tears were rolling down her cheeks now. "*L* is for the long-lost leader," she said.

It felt like a losing battle, but Finlay kept trying. "Remember the rejuvenation," he said.

"Aye, rejuvenation." Mary was smiling through her tears.

Hastily, Finlay spread a sheet onto the mattress. Then, "You don't want your tea to get cold," he said, patting the bed.

Surprisingly meekly, Mary sat on the bed and swung her feet up. Finlay placed the duvet on top of her and handed her her cup of tea. She took a sip. Maybe, just maybe, she would actually drink it all and then doze off. Finlay thought that was more likely if he wasn't in the room.

"I'm just going to get some more milk for mine," he said.

He closed the door softly behind him. Now what?

Then he remembered Squirrel, asleep on the sitting-room floor.

"Squirrel! Wake up!"

"Uh?" Squirrel sat up blearily. "Whasser time?"

"It's half past five."

"Must do my shift. Did I tell you I'd got a job? I'm on the Tesco trolleys."

"But, Squirrel, I'm worried about Mary."

"Aye, I know. She's away with the fairies."

"I'm worried she might hurt herself or set fire to the flat or something. Maybe she should be in hospital."

"Och, she'll be all right. But she should be having the tablets. Has she not been taking them?"

"I don't know. What tablets, anyway?"

"Carbo-something. She's not very keen on them."

"Should we try and find them?"

"No, you're best leaving that to the CPN."

"Who's that?"

"The community psychiatric nurse. You could try giving him a ring. Anyway, I must do my shift. I don't want to get fired after only two weeks."

"What time do you finish?"

"Midnight. But I'll drop by tomorrow and see how she is."

Finlay was sorry to see Squirrel go, especially because now he could hear Mary muttering inside her bedroom. It was quite a soft muttering, but his guess was that it wouldn't stay like that for long.

Should he phone someone? He didn't know who Mary's doctor was. What about this CPN person that Squirrel had mentioned? But where would the number be? In any case, he wasn't sure that he wanted to invite someone in authority around to Leo's hiding place—not without consulting her.

Leo. He must find Leo. She would know what to do.

Finlay crept to the front door. He didn't want to alert Mary that he was going out; she would just become agitated all over again. But as his hand touched the handle, Zigger bounded up to him. His lead was in his mouth.

"All right then, Zigger. Let's go walkies," Finlay whispered.

LEO
Running on the Cracks

"He'll come 'round to you," says Kim, yet again. "It was just the shock, I'm sure." She pours me out some more tea—it must be my sixth cup. I've lost track of how long I've been sitting in their kitchen.

"Anyway," says Jacqueline, "you've got us. We're not disowning you!"

They're being so nice to me. But they can't rub out the picture in my mind of the old man in the armchair and the look on his face. No, not a look exactly—not a proper expression; rather, the *absence* of an expression. It was as if he was looking straight through me, as if he couldn't see me.

I don't think I'd feel so hurt if he hadn't looked so like Dad. And now it's Dad I want to see. I want to talk to him, to shout at him even, "Why did you have to quarrel? Why were you so proud? Why couldn't you even teach me Chinese?"

But of course I can't talk to Dad. Instead, I ask Kim and Jacqueline, "Would it be hard for me to learn Chinese?"

"What kind? Mandarin or Cantonese?" asks Jacqueline.

I feel foolish. That was something Dad *did* explain—about the different languages—but I was never very interested. "Whatever kind you speak," I say. "Is that Cantonese?"

Kim laughs. "If you mean Jacqueline, it's bad Cantonese. She hardly speaks it at all."

"Well, it's your fault, Mum. You shouldn't be so good at English! Anyway, at least I'm better than the others."

Kim sighs. "I tried and tried to get them all to keep it up, but once they went to school, they only wanted to speak English."

"Stop grumbling! Look, you've got a willing pupil at last—you can teach Leo!"

"Do you really want to learn, Leo? Is it so you can speak to your grandfather?"

"Yes. I just thought . . ." My voice trails away as I try to picture the scene. All I can see is that nonlook on the old man's face.

"Actually, he doesn't speak Cantonese. He can understand it, but he speaks a different language—it's called Hakka. Lots of the old people from the countryside speak Hakka. My mum—your auntie Luli—grew up speaking it, but she changed to Cantonese when she got married."

"Oh." It's all rather confusing and daunting. Anyway, I bet Grandfather still wouldn't want to know me even if there were a hundred different Chinese languages and I spoke them all.

As if on cue, Auntie Luli shuffles into the kitchen. She smiles at me and does a chopstick mime.

"See? Who needs language?" says Jacqueline. "Yes, you will stay and eat with us, won't you, Leo?"

But seeing the old lady has reminded me of Mary. Poor, agitated Mary. Is she alone or is there a motley collection of friends with her, eating, drinking, and smoking away her benefit money? Squirrel had already arrived before I left.

I look at my watch. I can't believe it's after six already.

"I must get back," I say.

Jacqueline sees me down the stairs and gives me a hug. "Come again soon! And don't worry about Uncle Jing. I'll work on him!"

It's nearly dark outside. Shall I walk or take the bus? The bus is scarily public, but walking is longer and colder. And Mary will be missing me. Suddenly I really want to be with her again. So what if she's not a relation? She cares about me as much as if she was my grandmother. I shouldn't have stayed away for so long.

I turn left, toward the little square. Beyond it is the main road and the bus stop.

I glance across the road, at the last house in the row. That's where Grandfather's flat is. He must be back there now. Is he thinking about me?

There's a car parked outside it, and someone is sitting in the driver's seat.

Maybe one of the social workers from the elderly center has just dropped Grandfather back home—but no, it's too late for that; Jacqueline told me the center closed at about four thirty. The car is probably nothing to do with him.

I walk on.

I hear the car door opening. I won't look 'round. I won't speed up. It's nothing to do with me. I must stop being so jumpy all the time.

"Leonora!"

I know that voice.

And now I do look 'round, but only for a split second. That's enough. I know that flat hat and that man. It's Uncle John.

My legs spring into action, almost before my brain has time to give them the message. Run, run! Faster, faster! You've got away before, and you can get away again! Just don't run on the cracks and you'll be all right.

'Round the corner of the dark square. Which way now? Ahead is the main road, the bright lights, the bus stop. On my right are railings and a little gate. It's open!

He hasn't turned the corner yet. I make a quick decision.

Through the gateway, across the grass, under the bare sycamore tree. There are some dark bushes ahead—evergreens. I guess there'll be another gate behind them, the other side of the square.

The ground is soft, soggy, even. That's good—he can't hear my footsteps.

But I can hear his. They've rounded the corner. They're running past the gate!

Yes. I crouch behind a prickly bush with berries on it and wait, my heart thudding.

He's stopped. He's running back again.

No more footsteps. He must have seen the open gate. He must be here, in the grassy square. I can't see him, I can't hear him, but I know he's here somewhere.

What shall I do? Keep still and wait, or run again? I'm right beside the railings. There must be another gate, there must!

I can't see one. And I can't risk moving between the bushes. I'll have to climb over the railings here, where I'm hidden by the leafy branches. The railings aren't very high. I can do it.

If only I hadn't brought this bag with me. Shall I just dump it? No, it's got my sketchbook in it. I don't want him to find that. The bag won't fit between the railings, so I fling it over.

Now me! What to grasp? How to do it? Somehow, in an awkward mixture of hands, knees, and feet, I lever myself up. Now I'm standing at the top, wobbling, ready to jump. But a spike of the railings is caught inside my trouser leg. Still wobbling, I crouch and try to free it.

"Let me help you."

He's there, in front of me, the other side of the railings.

"No!"

It's too late. He's grabbed my knees. I'm toppling forward.

"Leonora, it's all right."

But it's not all right. Somehow I'm on my feet, on the pavement beside him, and he's got hold of my wrists, one in each hand. My bag is over his shoulder.

"Let me go!" My voice comes out as a fierce whisper. Should I shout? Scream? But what would he do then? And what would I say if someone did come?

"Don't be a silly girl. You know I wouldn't hurt you." His voice is horribly soft. He has that soppy smile on his face. "I've got some sandwiches in the car," he says.

"I don't want them. Go away!" Now my voice is rising.

His grip tightens. "I haven't done anything to you," he says, still in the same murmuring voice but without the smile. "I haven't done anything to anyone. And you're not to tell anyone that I have."

I've got to think of something! Suddenly it comes to me.

His car is parked nearly opposite the Yeungs' house. I'll let him take me toward it, then yell their names.

"Maybe I am a bit hungry," I say.

The smile is back. "There's a thermos of tea too," he says. "I know you like tea."

But he obviously doesn't trust me. He's still gripping one wrist as we walk back 'round the square toward Burn Street.

I must try to make him relax, lose his guard. If he loosens his grip, maybe I could even make a run for the Yeungs' front door. "How's Aunt Sarah?" I ask.

Does he hesitate a second?

"She's very worried about you, of course. We all have been."

"I'm sorry," I say. His grip remains tight.

I can see the car now. This is the moment.

"Jacqueline!" I shout. Why won't my voice come out louder? It's like one of those dreams where you can't make yourself heard. "Jacqueline! Kim! Andy!"

Now his hand is over my mouth. He's dragging me by one wrist toward the car.

I tug, struggle, kick. I try to pry off his fingers with my free hand. They're clamped tight.

"Don't make a silly fuss," he says. His face is right up to mine now. His mild-looking brown eyes are magnified behind his thick glasses.

His glasses! He can hardly see without them. I manage

to snatch them, then fling them into the road. Instinctively, he removes his hand from my mouth and reaches down to grope for them.

"Help!" I yell, and the hand is back.

"I've got another pair in the car," he mutters.

We're at the car now. The Yeungs haven't heard me.

But someone's coming, from the direction of the square.

"Leo!"

I can't believe it. It's Finlay. And not just Finlay. The dog is with him.

"Get him, Zigger!"

Zigger growls and makes a rush. He seizes Uncle John's trouser leg.

"Get him off!" Uncle John yells. He staggers and lets go of me.

"Quick, Leo!" Finlay takes my hand, and we're both running.

FINLAY
Escape

"This way!"

Finlay let go of Leo's hand. He hurtled ahead of her down a flight of stone steps.

So many steps! Don't speed up or you'll fall. Don't slow down or he'll find us.

They reached the bottom and turned the corner, out of view.

He couldn't hear the shouting anymore. Did that mean that Zigger had left off?

Ahead, cars raced over a concrete flyover.

"We're near that Chinese supermarket. There's a subway somewhere," he panted. Leo had caught up with him now. She looked so white.

Their footsteps echoed in the tunnel under the motorway. He was pretty sure there were only two sets of footsteps.

They emerged at the edge of a godforsaken stretch of litter-strewn grass. If only it wasn't so open! But at least the sky was dark now. A light rain was falling.

They ran past a deserted bench and a children's slide plastered with graffiti, toward some bleak-looking flats. Finlay looked wildly around for cover.

"Here." They darted into a passageway between two red-brick blocks. In the wall were cavities for enormous communal bins.

"I hope this isn't a dead end," he said, but they turned a corner and found themselves in a car park.

"Where's Zigger?" said Leo, panting by his side.

The same question had been nagging Finlay. "I expect he'll find us." He tried to sound more confident than he felt. They couldn't afford to slow down or turn back.

They followed a maze of small roads and alleyways

through a housing estate. Left, then right, then left, then right. Finlay tried to keep his sense of direction.

On and on they ran. His lungs felt like bursting. The red-brick houses and flats gave way to grander, older stone buildings with bay windows.

"We're in posh land now. There's a river near here."

"What, the Clyde?"

"No, the Kelvin."

A tall gate in some iron railings bore the notice KELVIN WALKWAY. They ran down a path that led them through woodland to a wider track beside the river.

"Let's stop here for a bit—I'm sure it's all right now."

They sat on a bench, the drizzle refreshing on their hot faces. The river glinted in the darkness. Finlay felt his heart thudding furiously and then beginning to slow down.

Neither of them said anything at first. They were listening, listening for footsteps, tense and wary as birds on a twig ready to fly at the slightest sound. But it was quiet here. Just distant traffic and the whirring of wings as two ducks rose from the water.

"My mum used to take me here to feed the ducks," he said at last. And then, "What happened? It was him, wasn't it?"

"Yes. He was sitting in his car outside my grandfather's house. He must have seen me come out from Jacqueline's. Oh, Finlay, now I can never go back there!"

"I bet *he* won't want to go back there. Zigger really went for him, didn't he?"

"But what's happened to Zigger?"

"I don't know." Again, Finlay tried to keep the worry out of his voice. "Maybe he'll catch us up."

They listened again. This time there was something—a jingling and a soft panting. "He has!"

But it was a different dog, a brown-and-white spaniel proudly bearing a stick as big and branching as a deer's antler. "Good evening," said the owner, nodding to them as they shrank back instinctively on their bench. Then dog and man passed, and there was silence again.

"Maybe Zigger's found his way back to Mary's by a different route," suggested Finlay.

"Oh, no! What if Uncle John follows him?"

"Don't you think he'd be more likely to be running *away* from Zigger?"

"I don't know. I don't know anything anymore. Oh, Finlay, he's got my bag! He's got all my sketches!"

"Well, at least he hasn't got you."

"I hate thinking about it. What if you hadn't turned up, Finlay!"

"But I did, didn't I?"

Finlay would have liked an outpouring of gratitude at this point, but he realized Leo was still in a state of shock.

"I thought you were going to have an evening in" was all she said.

He knew he had to tell her why he'd come to find her,

how ill Mary was, how they had to get some help for her. Maybe even get her into hospital. But it wasn't easy to start. Leo was supposed to be the capable, protective one, the one who would know what to do, but now she was in need of protection herself. Still, the Mary problem wasn't going to go away just because Leo's situation had got worse.

A squirrel ran out from a bush, froze, then approached them with small splay-legged steps and inquisitive eyes.

"They're really tame here," he said. "Everyone feeds them. Once one climbed onto Mum's shoulder." That felt like yesterday, yet it felt like a hundred years ago. The river, the autumn leaves, the squirrels, they were all just the same, but everything in his life had changed. Suddenly he wished he hadn't quarreled with Mum.

Leo reached out a hand to the squirrel, who investigated it, found it was empty, and retreated again. "That reminds me," she said in a flat voice. "Squirrel came 'round to Mary's today, just before I went out."

"I know. I've been 'round there," he said.

He had started now. He had to tell her sooner or later, and so out it all came.

To his relief, none of it was a huge surprise to Leo. "She's been getting more and more like that. I suppose I must have been growing used to it. Let's get back there now. Is it very far, Finlay?"

This was more like the old Leo, the Leo who knew what

to do. Finlay's heart lightened briefly, then fell again as he sensed what she must be thinking. If Mary went into hospital, where could Leo go?

LEO
The Hokey Cokey

I won't think about him. I mustn't, I can't bear to. I'll just think about Mary.

Here we go. We've reached her landing. My key—the one Mary copied for me—is in the lock. The flat is quiet for once.

"Ziggie boy!" Finlay whispers.

No dog comes bounding up. Finlay doesn't say anything, but he looks close to tears.

I squeeze his hand. "At least it looks like Mary's asleep," I say.

But no. Mary flings the bathroom door wide to greet us. "All my brothers and sisters have come!"

Her hair is frothy. She must have been washing it. But the bottles in her hand aren't shampoo bottles; they're small and brown. Her flimsy nightie is dripping wet.

"Mary, you'll catch cold. Do you want me to rinse your hair? Where's the towel?"

"It's with the others. They had to be together."

What's she on about?

"Maybe there's one in the bedroom," says Finlay. He goes to look.

"Are those pill bottles, Mary?"

In reply, she shakes them solemnly. They make no sound. They're empty.

"Mary, have you been swallowing them? How many did you take?"

She bursts out laughing. "The toilet's gonnae swallow them! In one gulp!"

I look into the loo. It's full of pills.

"But aren't they the ones your CPN said you had to take?"

"The CPN. The sea peahen. Did you see the sea peahen?" She cackles at her pun.

If only I could talk some sense into her! "No, you know I didn't see him. I had to hide in the wardrobe that time he came 'round, don't you remember? But you told me what he said. You mustn't stop taking the pills."

"He gave me the wrong message. That Lorraine must have been fiddling with the computer."

Finlay has found two towels. He wraps one 'round her.

Mary lets me rinse her hair in the basin. "You're good. You're looking after me," she says. The soap dish is full of cigarette ash, but I decide not to say anything.

I make the other towel into a turban for her. She's delighted with her reflection. "Now I'm the Queen of Arabia!"

"Shall I be your maid and get some nice warm clothes on you?"

But she's reluctant to tear herself away from the mirror. "Wait!" She's tearing a strip of loo paper from the roll. Now she's poking it up the tap.

"What are you doing?"

"Those who watch shall see." She dips the now-wet toilet paper into the ash-filled soap dish. Now she's smearing it on the mirror, trying to write something. It looks like a backwards *L*. "Mirror writing," she says. "That's how to get the right message to the other side."

"Mary, I think it's more important to get you warm."

She lets me lead her through to the bedroom. "It's in a bit of a mess," Finlay warns.

That's an understatement. Or maybe *mess* is the wrong word. Mary's bed is in the middle of the room, piled high with a pyramid of bedclothes and towels. The wardrobe door is wide open, and all her clothes are strewn on the floor around the bed. No, not strewn exactly—there's some kind of pattern to it. The sleeves of the dresses and cardigans have been spread out and are touching each other, like two concentric rings of people holding hands.

"It looks like the Hokey Cokey," says Finlay. I start to giggle—I can't help it. To my relief, Mary is joining in. But now her laughter is turning into tears.

"Don't cry, Mary. What is it?"

"The rings!" she says between great wild sobs.

I spot a cozy long-sleeved nightdress among the Hokey-Cokey players. And there's her tartan dressing gown. I hope Mary won't make a fuss if I remove them from the outer ring.

"Finlay, why don't you make some tea while I get Mary dressed."

I pick up the nightdress. She doesn't object. But what's this? There's a hole in it. It's a cigarette burn. Never mind, it'll still do.

"Arms up."

Mary raises them like an obedient child, and I slip the old damp nightie off her head, then rub her with the towel. She's skinnier than ever.

"You're good," she says again, the tears gone now. I help her into the new nightie, and she sticks a finger through the burn hole. "Do you see the ring?"

"Yes, and look, there's one in this dressing gown. Have you been smoking in bed, Mary? You know that's dangerous."

"It's the ring of fire!" she protests. "They all need it." She picks up one of the dresses, and I see that there's a burn in that too.

She's done it to all her clothes. She must have been doing it while Finlay was out, while we were escaping from . . . I don't want to think about Uncle John. I won't think about him. I must concentrate on Mary.

"Tea's ready!" calls Finlay from the kitchen.

"Rejuvenation!" says Mary, sounding more like her old self.

"I'll give you a hand," I call back to Finlay. I really need to talk to him about her. Can we sneak a few minutes on our own?

I take Mary into the sitting room and pick up some of the cushions, which are all over the place.

"You sit down, Mary. I'll help Finlay bring it in." I turn on the telly, though I know she won't be able to concentrate on it.

In the kitchen, Midget is brushing against Finlay's legs hopefully as he stirs sugar into Mary's big mug of tea.

"Where does she keep the pet food?" he asks. "I suppose it's under the floorboards or in the bath or somewhere mad like that."

"I see what you mean about her. She's definitely getting worse." I tell him about the burnt clothes. "What if she'd set fire to the flat?"

"She needs someone to look after her," he says.

"She likes it when I look after her. She keeps saying so; she keeps telling me I'm good."

"Yeah, but you can't do it—not all the time, not twenty-four hours a day. And her pals are hopeless. She should be in hospital."

But what about me? What would I do if she went? Could I stay here on my own? Where else could I go?

I won't think about me. I'll just think about Mary.

"How do you think she'd feel about hospital?" I say. "I mean, she's always hanging about that place, but she hardly ever talks about when she was in there herself."

"I don't think she'd be keen, somehow."

I feel the same. The way they all talk about "doing a runner" they make it sound like a prison.

"So what are we going to do?" I ask. "Phone someone, or what?"

"Squirrel said something about a CPN."

"Yes, but I don't know his number. And shouldn't we ask her first?"

"She'd never agree. She'd probably just go berserk—even berserker than she is already."

"But I don't like going behind her back. It feels like we're plotting against her. Wouldn't it be better if we could talk her into it?"

"Okay, then." Finlay still sounds doubtful.

I find an open tin of cat food in the fridge and hand it to him. "You do Midget, and I'll start on Mary."

Mary is wandering about the sitting room.

"Rejubilation!" she says when she sees the tea. She takes the cup and a biscuit, but I can't get her to sit down.

How shall I start? "Mary, I don't think you're very well."

"I'm not going in," she says.

I'm taken aback. I didn't think she'd get it so quickly. Then I realize other people must have had this conversation with her in the past. It's not going to be easy.

"But you need someone to look after you."

"They don't look after you. They look at you. They're at

it." She's pacing faster now. Some tea slurps out of the cup onto the floor.

"I'll come and visit you, Mary. I'll make sure they look after you."

"I need to be here. I need to tell the people. I need to pass on the message."

Pointless to ask what message. "Can't you pass it on to the people in there?" I suggest.

"They're all crazy in there!"

She dunks a biscuit in her tea, then waves it about. "*D* is for the dancing," she says.

"I'm sure it wouldn't have to be for long. Just till they get you back on the right medicine."

It was the wrong thing to say. "I'm no' taking it!" she says. "I'm no' taking the bitter pill. The devil can take the bitter pill."

I rack my brains. I remember the first time I met Mary, on that bench, waiting to see Ronnie and give him the chocolate Hob Nobs. "Ronnie's in there—you like him," I try.

She's not listening anymore. She's waving the biscuit about again. "I could bring you in some biscuits," I say.

Then I remember something else. There was a nurse with Ronnie, wasn't there? In a flash, his name comes to me.

"You like Jim Docherty, don't you?"

At last she's standing still. "Aye, Jim Docherty is good. Jim Docherty is the best. Aye, I like Jim Docherty."

"Jim would look after you."

"Aye, Jim would look after me. I like Jim Docherty. He's the best. He's the best of a bad bunch. He's not in the bunch. He's good."

Am I finally getting somewhere?

Finlay comes in. "Midget's being very polite. I think she's leaving half of it for Zigger," he says. "I wish he'd come back."

"Finlay, Mary was saying how much she likes Jim Docherty. Why don't we ring the hospital?"

FINLAY ■ ■ ■
Comings and Goings

"Jim's not on yet. He's doing nights this week. He'll be here in a couple of hours. Can I give him a message?"

Why was nothing ever simple? Finlay wondered. "Could you ask him to phone Mary McNally?"

"Who's speaking, please?"

"I'm . . . a friend of Mary's. I'm a bit worried about her."

"Is she there? Shall I speak to her? Tell her it's Yvonne."

"Mary, it's Yvonne. Will you speak to her?"

But Mary didn't think too much of this idea. "Yvonne didnae let me use the washing machine," she said.

Yvonne overheard and said something about not mixing whites and coloreds, which Finlay didn't feel was getting them very far. Then she offered, "I'll get Jim to call when he comes on. But if you're really worried about her, you should ring NHS 24. That's the proper procedure. If they think she sounds bad enough, they'll send the rota doctor out to assess her." She gave Finlay the number.

It sounded quick and simple, but it wasn't. The evening slipped into night as they phoned, explained, waited, talked Mary back into it, answered the phone, explained again, waited again.

Leo packed a bag for Mary and kept her as calm as possible. "But I can't face seeing the doctor," she told Finlay. "I'm sorry. It's because of *him*. You know."

"The bird man!" said Mary. It was funny how she could still be so quick off the mark.

"If he's told the police I gave him the slip, then I bet my picture will be in the paper again, maybe even tomorrow. No one must see me here."

Finlay didn't really see why not. She probably wouldn't be able to stay here anymore once Mary had gone—or would she? "Okay," he said, but when the doorbell rang and she went off to hide in the wardrobe, he wished he'd tried to dissuade her. Even with his skill at fabrication, he wasn't sure how he'd explain his presence in Mary's life.

The doctor was small, gray, and tired looking. If he was surprised to find a thirteen-year-old boy in atten-dance, he didn't show it. He listened politely to what Mary had to say about messages, leadership, and dancing, then asked her to count backward from a hundred, subtracting seven each time. She obliged with "ninety-seven, eighty-five, ten to five, half past six." When he asked her to name some common animals, she came up with "cat, dog, all my family."

The doctor was convinced, and he phoned for an ambulance.

As soon as he went, Mary snapped out of her compliant mood. "They can't get me!" she said. "They're at it. You're at it too!"

"I'm not. I just want you to be safe."

"I'm leaving!"

Leo had reappeared. "Mary, you can't."

"I can. I do. I will. I can conquer." She marched toward the front door. Her hand was on the handle.

The phone rang.

"It's Jim Docherty, Mary."

She hovered, hesitated, then took the receiver.

"Jim, they want me to go in. I won't go. I'm counting on you, Jim. I'm counting backwards. You're the best, Jim."

Finlay couldn't hear what Jim said, but it did the trick. After the phone call there was no more talk of escape. Instead, she paced around the room, saying, "Jims are good, and Ronnies are good," over and over until the bell rang and Leo hid again.

The two young ambulance drivers introduced themselves as Paula and Paige.

Luckily, Mary took to them. "You're not Jims or Ronnies, but you're goodly," she said.

"Have you got a coat, pet?" asked Paula. "Have you got a bag, pet?" asked Paige, and then, turning to Finlay, "Are you a relation?"

Finlay had considered being a grandson from the country, but Mary told them, "He's Sherlock. He's my pal."

"Do you want to come with her in the ambulance?"

Finlay hadn't thought of this. He couldn't really go with Mary and leave Leo. "No—no, I've got to get home."

"Shall I phone for a taxi?"

"No, it's okay, it's just 'round the corner."

Paula switched out all the lights.

"Have you got your keys, love?" Paige was leading a surprisingly meek Mary out onto the landing. Finlay and Paula followed.

The door of flat 2/2 opened, and Dressing Gown appeared. She eyed the company with a look that said "I saw this coming."

"I can take the cat in," she said. "I did last time."

"Or I could come and feed her," said Finlay.

Dressing Gown gave him a funny look. "You stick to your paper round," she said.

"He's a detective," said Mary.

"Yes, dear," said Paige, and started to lead Mary down the stairs.

"Someone from social work will probably come 'round

tomorrow to make sure it's secure and to sort out about the cat," said Paula to Dressing Gown.

Outside, the ambulance gleamed white in the dark street. Finlay felt a wrench as Mary climbed in.

"Have a nice time," he said. That sounded stupid. "I'll come and visit."

He waved and set off as if for home.

At the corner, he waited till he heard the ambulance drive off. He waited some more—long enough, he hoped, for Dressing Gown to stop nosing about and get back to bed. Then he crept back and up the stairs.

"Leo," he whispered through the letter box.

She let him in. The flat was still dark. Officially it was empty. Dressing Gown mustn't see any light under the door.

She mimed for him to take off his shoes, and they padded through to the sitting room, where just the table lamp was switched on. "I'm so glad you came back," she said.

"Did you think I wouldn't?"

Her face crumpled. Tears came. Her body shook with sobs. She flung herself onto the sofa and lay there, heaving.

Finlay had seen Leo cry before, that evening at the Yeungs', but not in this uncontrollable way. He didn't know if she was crying for herself or for Mary, and he didn't ask. He didn't feel embarrassed the way he normally would. He knelt on the floor beside her, took her dangling hand, and felt a return squeeze.

The sobs subsided. She sat up. "There's so much to think about, isn't there?" she whispered.

"Yes. But I feel sort of dazed."

"You're tired. You'd better go home."

"I'm not going home," Finlay said. "Not tonight. I'm not leaving you on your own."

"But what about your mum and dad?"

"I'll ring them. I'll make something up. But not this second."

They sat in silence. Midget padded in, jumped onto Finlay's lap, and began kneading and purring. Finlay thought about Dressing Gown and the social worker who was supposed to call tomorrow. But he felt too tired to talk about that now. "We'd better get up early" was all he said.

"We've got our paper rounds anyway."

"Hey, Midget, what's up?" The cat had tensed, stopped purring. Her ears were pointing backward as if she was listening to something.

Then they heard it too. The click of claws on the stone staircase and the trailing of a lead.

With an exchanged glance but no words, they went to the front door. Finlay opened it a crack, and Zigger came bounding in.

"Hello, is that Rab?"

"Yes."

"This is Finlay Grant's mother."

"Well, tell him to get out of bed and get down here."

"So he's not with you?"

"No, and neither is that pal of his. And Scott Paterson's already doing a double round—I'm gonnae have to do the Z run myself. WHIT DO YOU MEAN, YOU'VE LOST YOUR BAG? These kids don't bloody care. Mind you, that wee lassie's maistly dead reliable. Must be your son's influence. I expect they're painting each other's fingernails. Whit time did he set off?"

"That's just it—he didn't. We haven't seen him since yesterday after school. I'll have to phone the police again."

"That's a bit drastic, if you ask me. IF YOU LOSE THIS ONE, I'M TAKING IT OFF YOUR WAGES. Your son's most likely carousing with his pals. Have you tried that Chinese lassie?"

"I don't know who you mean."

"Emma Clark. NO, YOU CAN'T HAVE MONDAY OFF. Aye, Emma Clark. She's a nice enough wee girl, if she'd just wash that clown paint off her face. I DON'T CARE IF YOU'RE GOING TO THE MOON FOR THE WEEKEND, I WANT YOU HERE ON MONDAY MORNING. Is she no' in your son's class?"

"I've never heard of her, but I can ask the school. He did say something about a Chinese girl."

"Aye, well, I can't hang around. I'm behind as it is. NOT SO FAST, YOUNG FOWLER—WHAT HAPPENED TO MRS. SPURWAY'S *TIMES* YESTERDAY? I'll let you know if he turns up here."

"Well, thank you anyway."

"And if he turns up at your end, give his neck an extra wring from me."

LOST PROPERTY

"Hello? Is that Mrs. . . . er, Yeung?"

"It's Jacqueline Yeung."

"Ah. I believe I have some lost property belonging to you."

"Lost property?"

"A bag."

"I'll buzz you up."

⁕ ⁕ ⁕

"This is the bag. Does it belong to someone who lives here?"

"I . . . sorry, where did you find this bag?"

"I saw a young lady come out of this house last night, and she dropped it. I tried to alert her attention, but she seemed very nervous. She ran off. I would have come 'round straight-away, but it was getting late and I didn't want to disturb you."

"Oh, well, yes, I think the bag belongs to . . . a friend of mine. She was in a bit of a hurry to catch the bus. If you leave it here, I can give it back to her."

"So the young lady doesn't live here?"

"No, she . . . why do you want to know? You're not—"

"Yes, I think you know who I am, and I think we both know who the young lady is. She's my niece, Leonora, isn't she?"

"Sorry, I don't know who you're talking about. I don't know anyone called Leonora."

"That's what she's told you to say, isn't it?"

"What do you mean? I said I don't know this Leonora person."

"Perhaps she's even told you some things about her background which may have misled you. But you do need to understand that my niece is a very vulnerable young person. She was in an extremely emotional state when she was in our care—"

"Look, none of this is anything to do with me."

"It's a little late for playing games. Leonora is on the Missing People register. Anyone knowingly harboring her without notifying the police is committing a criminal offense."

"We're not harboring anyone. Please go away."

"And setting dogs on people is another crime."

"Dogs? We don't have a dog. Oh, hi, Mum. It's okay, this man just . . . got the wrong house."

"I did not get the wrong house. You told me yourself that the bag belonged to a friend who had left your house to catch a bus."

"Hey, that's Leo's bag! It's got all her pictures in it!"

"Mum!"

"Ah, just as I thought. So is Leonora staying here, or is she across the road with her grandfather?"

"No, she's—"

"Don't tell him anything, Mum!"

"I think your daughter is a little over-excited. But I'm sure you'll be more reasonable. I simply need to know where Leonora is living."

"Sorry, I made a mistake."

"You can tell me. I want to help her. Where can I find Leonora?"

"My mum doesn't know what you're talking about. You'd better go now. I'll take the bag."

"I don't think that's such a good idea, after all. I'll keep it. It may contain some important clues."

LEO
The Intrusion

The phone wakes me, or rather Zigger, who is barking at it the way he always does when it rings.

"Shut up, Zigger," says a bleary voice. Finlay is sprawled on some cushions on the floor. What's he doing here? Then I remember.

The phone stops as I dislodge Midget from my chest

and sit up. Bright low sunlight is flooding into Mary's sitting room. My watch says it's ten thirty. How could I have slept so long?

"Finlay! We've missed our paper rounds."

Finlay sits up. He's alarmed. But not about the paper round. "Someone's at the door!" he hisses.

Zigger's in the hall now, barking ferociously at the front door. A woman's voice floats through the letter box: "Hello! Hello! Is anyone there? Good dog," And then a man's voice, like an echo: "Good dog. Good dog."

"It's the social workers," whispers Finlay.

How does he know? And what shall we do? Hide? Answer the door? We do neither, just sit frozen helplessly as we listen to the voices saying "hello" and "good dog" again.

Zigger has stopped barking now, maybe soothed by all the praise.

A key turns in the lock. "There's a good dog!" The woman's voice sounds a little nervous this time, as we hear the door open.

More barking, but instead of the low, threatening kind it's the friendly paws-on-chest kind. And now Zigger is racing through to tell us about his new friends.

They follow him into the room, see us, and blink.

The woman looks more like a student than a social worker, with her long, messy hair, jeans, and shoulder bag. "I didn't think anyone was here. I'm the duty social worker from the hospital." She sounds more apologetic than accusing. "And Terry here is a trainee."

A gangly young man says, "Hiya," and then starts stroking Midget, who is basking in a shaft of sunshine.

"We're Mary's friends," says Finlay. "We were here when the ambulance came—well, I was. We just thought we'd stay and kind of . . . make sure the cat was all right."

"Is this your dog?" asks the woman.

"No," I say. "Yes," says Finlay.

She looks confused. She rummages in the shoulder bag and consults an official-looking sheet of paper. "So Miss McNally just has the one cat, is that right? It says here that she's given permission for a neighbor to feed it."

"Or we could, if you like?" suggests Finlay. "We're Mary's friends. We could keep an eye on things till she's back from hospital."

Nice try, Finlay.

The social worker smiles. "It's kind of you to offer," she says. "Sorry, I don't know your names. I'm Rachel, by the way."

Finlay glances at me, then mutters "Finlay."

"Emma," I say, without meeting her eye.

Is it my imagination, or is she giving me a haven't-I-seen-you-before look? But she says, "I'm sorry, Finlay and Emma, but we can't give you access to the flat. In fact, we're going to have to turf you out. We've got to make sure it's secure before I hand the keys to the council." A thought seems to occur to her. "Is there just the one set of keys?"

I hope I'm not looking guilty as Finlay says, "How should we know?"

"Well, it's just that usually the ambulance drivers wouldn't let anyone who wasn't a resident stay in the flat." She gives her apologetic smile again, aware that she's hinting that we let ourselves in. How will Finlay get out of this one?

"Oh, well, they didn't realize that Emma was here, and then I came back to make sure she was all right," says Finlay. The truth for once, or near enough.

"I see." I don't think she does, but she probably wants to get this job over with. "Well, Terry and I will just check the other rooms—make sure there's no one hiding in the wardrobe!"

She's joking. I smile wanly, thinking of all the times I was cooped up in the darkness, my nose pressed up against Mary's flimsy charity-shop dresses.

"The bedroom's a bit of a mess," says Finlay. The same could be said of him. His hair is sticking in all directions, and his clothes are crumpled from sleeping in them. He follows the two social workers on the tour of inspection, with Zigger bounding after them.

I dress hastily. I suppose I'd better pack too. All my possessions are in the bottom of Mary's corner cupboard, except for the nylon hold-all I brought with me. I suppose Uncle John must still have that. I try not to think about him.

My unused school bag is still here, with all the books and gym kit. I never disposed of it, as it seemed too risky, and now I hesitate. Shall I leave it? No, better take it. I don't want any social-work or council people finding it here. As I thrust my few other things inside it, I remember the first day of term and setting off with Flo and Caitlin for the school I never reached.

I'd planned that getaway, but I haven't planned this one. Where am I going to go?

Finlay and the social workers come back in. Rachel glances at my bag and looks worried. "Shouldn't you two be at school?" she says.

"We're just going," says Finlay.

"But what about the dog?"

"We'll drop him off at my house on the way."

Her expression is more and more doubtful. "Do your parents know about all this? Maybe we should phone them."

"It's okay, they're expecting me," lies Finlay. Rachel glances at me, and he goes on, "And Emma's parents know too. They're pals of my mum and dad, actually."

"Well, we'd better just take a note of your full names and contact details anyway. Do you want to take them down, Terry?" She hands him the official bit of paper and, ever apologetic, says, "Sorry to sound like the police—it's just something we have to do."

Finlay says, "Finlay Grant, 58 Tiverton Road." He's so good at bluffing that I don't know if it's his real address or not. I say "Emma Clark, 43 Beechgrove Crescent." Beechgrove

Crescent is a real road—it's on my paper round—but the numbers only go up to 39.

As Terry finishes writing, the phone rings again. Rachel answers it.

"Who?" she says. "Leo? No, there's no Leo here." She gives us a questioning glance, and we both shake our heads hard. "I think you must have got the wrong number."

Who was that? Jacqueline, I suppose.

"Come on then, Zigger." Finlay's in a hurry now. He doesn't fancy any more questions, nor do I.

A newspaper is protruding from the letter box. Rab must have found someone to do Finlay's round this morning. Finlay takes it. I sneak a quick glance at the headline—something about the bin man. At least I'm not on the front page.

"I'll bring this in to Mary when we visit her," says Finlay.

Rachel looks quite relieved to see us go. "Good-bye, then. We'll just stay and tidy up a bit, and then we'll sort out about the cat with the neighbor."

So this is it. We're out in the street. I'm a runaway again.

TAXI DRIVER

"Excuse me—"

"Shall I put that bag in the boot, sir?"

"No, thank you. Actually, I don't need a taxi. I was just wondering if I could ask for some help."

"Ask away."

"How well do you know Glasgow?"

"I've only driven all about the place every day fur the last twenty-five years."

"I've got some sketches here. . . . Would you mind taking a look?"

"Go on, then—I'm no' buying any dirty pictures off you, mind."

"No, they're perfectly innocent. Could you look at this one?"

"That wee moggie could do with going on a diet."

"I meant the other picture."

"Is that no' the canal? Aye, it looks like the Forth and Clyde Canal."

"You don't recognize the bridge?"

"That wee swing bridge? Wait a minute. I'd say it's the one by Glennie Avenue. I dropped a couple of lassies off near there the other night. Both pished—I thought they were going to throw up in the cab."

"Glennie Avenue, did you say?"

"Aye. Do you want a lift there?"

"No, thank you, I've got the car. But here—take this, you've been most helpful."

"Nae bother."

"This is where I first saw you," said Finlay to Leo. He threw a stick along the towpath, and Zigger scooted after it.

"When I was the archenemy," said Leo.

They had headed from Mary's to the little swing bridge without exchanging a word, as if by some joint instinct.

Zigger returned the stick and started barking at some ducks.

"Finlay, why did you tell that social worker he was yours? He's Ronnie's."

"Yes, but Ronnie's in hospital. They'd have put him in some horrible kennels or something. Anyway, I don't think Ronnie really wants him."

"But what will your parents say?"

Finlay shrugged and said nothing, though the same question was weighing heavily on him. He threw the stick again for Zigger. The ducks had swum away.

"You didn't phone them last night, did you?"

Why did Leo have to rub everything in?

"I was going to—you know I was. It's just that Zigger turning up like that put it out of my mind."

"Well?"

"Well, what?"

"Your mum and dad—you'd better phone them now. They'll be worried stiff. There's a phone box on the corner."

"Oh, stop nagging me. You sound just like Mum. Anyway, it's you we're meant to be talking about, not me. Where are you going to go?"

"I don't know."

"You could go back. You've got your key still, haven't you?"

"Yes, but I haven't got the extra deadlock key. Anyway, I don't want to stay there on my own. Not with Dressing Gown and social workers and council people prowling 'round."

"How about Jacqueline's?"

"I can't."

"What, just because it's a bit cramped? I bet they'd put you up till you'd sorted something else out."

"It's not that. It's because of Uncle John. He saw me coming out from that house, and he knows my grandfather's address too. He'll be lurking 'round that street again. I can't go back there."

"But you could tell them about him. How he tried to force you into his car—that's bang out of order, even if he is your uncle. They could report him to the police, or you could."

"I've thought about that. But supposing the police believed him and not me? And anyway, maybe he's reported *me* to them already. Maybe he's reported you too, for setting a dog on him. We're probably both in the paper."

"Let's have a look." Finlay opened Mary's paper with its

BIN KILLER CAUGHT! headline and flicked through it. "There doesn't seem to be anything," he said.

"Not yet."

"Well. . . ." Finlay wasn't going to give up. "I suppose I could ask Mum and Dad if you could stay with us."

"Aren't they a bit too law-abiding for that?"

"Or there's Ross McGovern. . . ." His voice petered out. For once he felt defeated.

"Finlay, I do think you should go home." Leo's voice was gentler now; she must be trying not to nag. "Never mind about me. I'll sort something out."

"I know!" Finlay jumped up. "We'll phone Marina."

"Tell her to hop on the seventy-three and get off at Sperry Street. I'll be waiting at the bus stop."

Good old Marina. That was her all over—a snappy decision instead of a whole lot of questions.

The bus stop was next to the phone box. An elderly couple stood there, and behind them a mother with a child in a pushchair.

"I'll wait with you," said Finlay.

"No, don't. I'll be fine. You *must* go home now."

"Well"—Finlay was reluctant, but then Zigger started snarling at the little boy, or rather at his stripy hat—"all right. I'll phone you as soon as I get the chance."

It was only a short walk from the bus stop to his house, but Finlay felt as if he was leaving one world and entering another. He'd been trying to keep Mum out of his thoughts, but he couldn't do it any longer. Would she be in? Would she be angry? How angry?

"Finlay! Where have you been?" She didn't look angry. She looked overjoyed. He felt a pang of guilt.

"I'm sorry, Mum." He returned her hug awkwardly, and Zigger tried to join in.

"Whose dog is this?" Now she was half laughing, half crying. "Get him off me!"

"It's okay, he only does that to people he likes. Down, Zigger!"

"Oh, Finlay, I'm so glad you're all right. Why didn't you phone us? We've been so worried."

"Sorry, I meant to. Can Zigger come in? It's okay, he likes cats—well, usually, anyway." Finlay tried to sound more optimistic than he felt as he saw their cat Mungo streak upstairs and felt Zigger straining on the lead.

Mrs. Grant wiped away a tear and tried to regain her composure. "Well, I don't know . . . just for now, then."

In the kitchen, Zigger immediately discovered Mungo's unfinished cat food and wolfed it down.

"How about you?" asked Mum. "Are you hungry?"

"Yes." Finlay realized he'd been living off cups of tea since four o'clock yesterday afternoon, and it must be lunchtime now.

"I saved some lasagna for you." Why was she being so

nice? Was it the calm before the storm? Finlay sat down at the table, and Zigger came and sat at his feet expectantly.

Mum put the dish in the microwave. "I'd better tell the police you've turned up," she said.

"The police—you haven't told them, have you?"

"Of course we have. Finlay, what did you think we'd do? Or didn't you think at all?" This was more like the old Mum. "If you'd stayed away another night, they were going to make a poster about you. You'd have been an official Missing Person."

"*I* would?" That struck Finlay as ironic.

"What are you looking like that for? It's not funny."

"No, I know. Sorry, Mum. I'm really sorry."

"Dad's been out looking for you all morning. I've only just persuaded him to go into work."

Zigger, sensing the rising tension, stood up and growled at Mum.

"Stop it, Zigger," said Finlay, though actually it was gratifying to have someone on his side for once.

"So where were you? Rab said something about a Chinese girl. Is this her dog?"

"A Chinese girl?" He feigned surprise while his mind raced over various possible explanations, all of them implausible.

Mum sighed. "Well, let's not have a repeat of yesterday. Just eat up now, and the explaining can wait."

Finlay agreed readily. He shoveled the lasagna into his mouth with Zigger-like speed.

"That nice girl Ailsa phoned last night," said Mum.

"Was it about her sweatshirt?" asked Finlay and then wished he hadn't.

"No, I don't think so. It was something to do with joining a band. She sounded really upset when I told her you'd gone missing."

"Why did you have to go and tell her that?" Finlay reacted with automatic irritation, and then, when Mum looked pained, said, "I'm sorry. Actually, I'm a bit tired. Maybe I should have a lie down."

It wasn't really true. He was playing for time, but Mum swallowed it and even allowed Zigger to go up to the bedroom with him. The dog lay on the floor guarding Finlay in case Mum showed any signs of turning fierce.

He lay there trying to plan what he would say to Mum when the time came, but it was hard to concentrate. Above his bed, Rick Reaper stared arrogantly down at him from the huge poster of Breakneck. As Finlay stared back, the tune of "Stone Sacrifice" started to play itself in his head. He'd gone off Breakneck a bit, but he still coveted Rick Reaper's black-and-silver guitar. It was a shame that his doughnut savings weren't mounting up the way he'd planned. And now he might get fired for missing his paper round.

Thinking about doughnuts and paper rounds made him

wonder how Leo was getting on with Marina and Kenny. She must be there by now.

Somehow his thoughts were getting muddled up with the "Stone Sacrifice" tune, and with other thoughts about Mary and Jacqueline and Uncle John. . . . Finlay drifted off to sleep.

LEO ▨ ▨ ▨ ▨
An Encounter

"Girl," says the little boy at the bus stop, pointing at me from his pushchair. "Girl, Mummy."

"Don't point—it's rude," says his mother, but now it seems to me that she keeps giving me sidelong glances. And that old couple have turned 'round to have a quick look too. Are they wondering about the school bag? Maybe they remember the description of it from the news reports. Maybe I should have left it at Mary's after all.

Apart from the child, they've all looked away now, but I still feel uncomfortable. Will I ever get used to ordinary people in public places again?

My bus, the one to Marina's house, isn't due for another twenty-five minutes. I'll go back to the canal and wait there. You can see the bus stop from the swing bridge, through the gap in the hedge.

The ducks are back too, now that Zigger is safely out of

the way. I wish I had some bread for them. I think about the loaves of bread Mary threw for the swans that day when I first met her, and I wonder how she is now. Did she sleep at all last night, and if so, how did she feel waking up in the hospital?

I can't help feeling nervous about meeting this Marina and her husband Kenny, even though Finlay has given Marina a good report: "She likes a laugh, and she knows how to keep her mouth shut." She didn't ask many questions on the phone, but when I arrive she's bound to have a few. How much should I tell them? And how long will they let me stay?

He's so quiet that I don't hear him till he's almost at the bridge.

"Hello again."

He's standing there, blocking the way.

No use crossing the bridge away from him: There's no towpath on the other side.

No use hoping for Finlay and Zigger to come to my aid again.

As if he can read my thoughts, he says, "So, no hell dog this time?"

Was he lurking, spying on us, waiting till Finlay was at a safe distance?

I'll have to humor him.

"I'm sorry about the dog," I say.

"And I'm sorry if I scared you last night." He's smiling.

He sounds polite, but he looks terrible. His raincoat is full of creases, and there is a brown blood stain on his ripped trouser leg. His face is gray with stubble, and his wispy hair looks wild. (No hat, I notice—did Zigger dispose of it?) Behind the thick glasses—so he did have a spare pair—his eyes have a crazed look.

How did he find me?

Again he seems to read my mind.

"You're quite a talented artist, you know," he says. "You really captured this scene."

So that's it. My drawings have given me away.

"I expect you'd like the sketchbook back, wouldn't you? And the bag too."

"Well. . . ."

Where is the bag? It's not over his shoulder. This is some kind of trap.

"It's in the car. Shall we go and get it?"

"It's all right. You can keep it. I don't really need it."

"Don't worry," he says. "I've changed my mind. I'm not going to force you to go back with me. I understand—you need time. Just come to the car, and I'll give you the bag."

I don't believe a word of it.

I glance at my watch and then at the bus stop. A quarter of an hour to go. Oh, why didn't I stay there with the little boy and his mother? Or why didn't I let Finlay wait with me?

"Come on." He steps back from the bridge and holds out a hand.

What shall I do? Can I somehow humor him for fifteen minutes and then make a run for the bus?

"I've changed my mind too," I say. Is this going to work or will he see straight through it? "I'm tired of being on the run. I'll go with you after all."

I can't tell from his smile whether he believes me or is just pretending to.

"Good girl," he says.

I step off the bridge. To my relief, he doesn't grab my wrist this time.

"I just need to pack a few things."

"You seem to have packed quite a lot already," he says, indicating the school bag.

"Yes, but there's some more stuff in the flat where I've been staying. It's very near here—it won't take long."

"Who have you been staying with?" he asks. I can tell he's not keen to meet anyone.

"No one. It's an empty flat—I've been squatting there."

He's still not happy. "Don't worry about your things," he says. "I can buy you some nice new things."

"No. I want my stuff. It's important to me."

"Well, you'll have to be quick. I've left the birds for too long as it is."

Where now? My mind is racing. I need to make a choice quickly. We're walking in the direction of Mary's flat, but I don't really have to take him there. I could just keep him walking and talking and then try to give him the slip when I sense he's off guard.

But I'm afraid that wouldn't work. He's sticking very close to me. Maybe I could try and smash his glasses again? I glance up at them, and now I see that they're attached to a string 'round his neck. So he's one jump ahead.

"You like the birds, don't you?" he's saying now, his voice right beside my ear as we walk.

"Yes, they're lovely."

"And you like me, really. I know you do."

What if I actually go to the flat? Are those social workers still there? Perhaps I should tell them everything. Surely they wouldn't make me go back with him?

But what if they believed him and not me? He looks pretty wild at the moment, but I know how smooth and convincing he can sound.

"I'm glad I've found you," he says. "I didn't want them to find you first."

What does he mean?

We're turning the corner into Struan Drive.

"They're all a bit hysterical," he carries on. "They're making up silly stories. You can tell them none of them are true. You will tell them, won't you?"

This doesn't make any sense to me, but I say yes just to keep him happy.

"Good girl," he says. "That's best for you. We don't want anything to happen to you, do we?"

What sort of threat is that? Is he even more dangerous than I suspected?

We're nearly at the flats. I slow down and glance up. There's no light on in Mary's sitting-room window, but I can't remember if it was on when Finlay and I left. Are the social workers still there?

"Is this it?" he asks.

"Yes." Too late to change my mind now.

We're on the echoey stone staircase.

And we're not alone. Someone's coming down the stairs.

I never thought I'd be so pleased to see the President.

"Hiya! Mary's oot," he says when he sees me. Then he turns over his shoulder. "It's the Prospect's pal! It's that Leo lassie."

"Delighted." The Godfather, close behind him, raises a hand in greeting.

The President stops a couple of stairs above us. "Who's the wee man?" he asks me.

Uncle John does grasp my wrist now. He pulls me to the wall of the staircase, to let them past. "Just ignore them. They look unsavory," he says.

"Let go of me," I say loudly.

He doesn't, but immediately the President is on my side.

"You heard what she said," he says.

"Please be on your way and mind your own business." The grip tightens.

The President takes a step down. I can smell his beery breath as he says, "Take your greasy paw off the lassie."

"She's my niece, and she needs my protection."

"Whose protection do you want, Leo, hen? His or oors?"

"Yours!"

The President lurches forward to grab the lapel of Uncle John's raincoat. But the alcohol is slowing his movements. Uncle John bats the hand away, then pushes him hard. The President loses his balance. Now he's sitting slumped on the stair above us.

"Let's get away from these people," says Uncle John. He starts to pull me down the stairs.

"Help me!" I yell, and then his free hand clamps over my mouth, just like that other time.

"It'll be much better for you if you don't make a silly fuss," he says under his breath.

He's dragging me out of the building. Has the President given up?

Someone overtakes us. It's not the President. It's the Godfather.

"Excuse me," he murmurs. As always, he sounds like the perfect gentleman.

Then he wrests both of Uncle John's hands off me, swings him 'round, and punches him in the stomach.

I don't see what happens next because I'm running and running, hoping I can still catch that bus.

FINLAY
Cornered

"Finlay. Dad's home." Mum brought in a cup of tea. "Drink this and come down."

It was evening already. Maybe he could get away with closing his eyes and going back to sleep again; as likely as not his parents would leave him undisturbed till morning. But he wanted to get this thing over with.

"Just coming." He had half formed a story. It was another lie, of course, but it had to be, for Leo's sake, and after today he would try to incorporate a little more blameless purity into his life.

Zigger stood to attention, tail wagging, as Finlay struggled to his feet.

"You'd better stay here, Ziggy boy," Finlay told him. Somehow he didn't think Dad and Zigger would hit it off straightaway.

Mum and Dad were in the sitting room. There were no hugs this time.

"Where the hell have you been?" asked his father.

"Chill, Dad," Finlay found himself answering instinctively,

though he knew this was the one expression guaranteed to rile his father and produce the opposite result.

Here it came: "I will not 'chill,' as you call it. You're lucky I'm not thumping you. Mum's been off her head with worry, you stupid little—"

"Steve, I think Finlay's going to explain." Mum put a calming hand on Dad's arm.

"Go on, then. But it had better be good."

"Well, I had this row with Mum. About what happened last night—no, the night before. I know it was mostly my fault,"

"Oh, very magnanimous," muttered his father, and "Wait, Steve," said his mother.

"Anyway, I went off to . . . to a friend's house."

"What friend?"

"You don't know them."

"Stop being so evasive. What friend?"

"Was it a Chinese girl?" asked Mum. "This one Rab's been telling us about—Emma Clark?"

Finlay hesitated. "Yes," he said.

"So who is she? How come we've never heard of her?"

"I don't have to tell you about every single person I ever meet, do I?" said Finlay, unwisely raising his voice. From upstairs, a sharp yapping started up.

"And on top of everything, you pick up a bloody dog!" his father shouted, thereby increasing the volume of the yapping.

"Look, let's go back to the Chinese girl," said Mum. "I think you must have been seeing her the night before as well. Were you, Finlay? Is she your girlfriend? Did you think we'd be cross with you for having a girlfriend?" In fact, she looked quite pleased.

"No, she's not really a girlfriend, but . . . but I thought you'd think she was." This was working out better than he'd hoped. "I didn't think you'd want me to be seeing her, or to go to her house. And then we were watching these DVDs, and it somehow got really late, and her mum said it would be all right to stay the night."

"So why didn't you phone?"

"Well, I tried to, but it was always engaged. Maybe it was when you were phoning 'round and phoning the police and things."

His parents were both looking thoughtful rather than incredulous. Was he on home ground now?

Not quite.

"So what about this morning? Why didn't you phone then? Why did you miss your paper round? Why weren't you at school?"

Finlay tried to produce one of the weary sighs he was usually so good at, but it didn't come out quite right. "I can only answer one question at a time," he said.

"This isn't the time for your cheeky retorts!" His dad looked as if he was about to jump out of his seat, but again one of Mum's calming pats restrained him.

"I've got a different question," she said. "Is Emma in your class?"

"Er. . . ." Finlay tried to remember what he had told Rab. "Yes," he said.

"Well, that's funny, because when I rang the school—"

"No, no, I mean, she's in my *year* but not my actual class. I forget which class she's in."

"What I was going to say was they said there was no Emma Clark on the school roll."

"That's probably because she's new." Finlay was blustering, and they knew it. Mum was shaking her head now, in a sad kind of way. "We just want the truth, Finlay. What's so hard about that? We know this girl exists—Rab told us. So who is she, and how do you know her?"

"And when are you going to give her back her bloody dog?" added Dad.

"Actually, I was wondering about the dog. . . . I mean, well, Emma's little sister has found that she's allergic to dogs. They've done these tests. So they can't keep the dog."

"NO, WE ARE NOT HAVING THE BLOODY DOG!"

Zigger started up again, his yapping turning into loud barks, and Finlay could hear him scrabbling at his bedroom door.

It was all going wrong. If only he could tell them the truth.

The phone rang. Let it not be that hospital social worker, Finlay prayed.

Mum answered it. "Yes . . . yes. I see. A Chinese girl,

yes. Leo? I thought it was Emma. . . . A meeting? Yes, I think that's a very good idea. Yes, all right, tomorrow evening, then."

She put the phone down. "That was Marina. She wants everything out in the open."

LEO
Persuasion

"Over to you, then, Leo," says Marina.

I've agreed to this. I've agreed to tell them all everything. "All" is Finlay and his parents, Jacqueline, Kim, Marina, and her husband Kenny. All eight of us are crammed into Marina and Kenny's cozy little sitting room.

I'm not sure where to start. Finlay has already heard most of my story, of course—well, he's been a huge part of it. Jacqueline knows a lot, and the others have been told bits and pieces, except for Finlay's mum and dad. If I know Finlay the way I think I do, they're still completely in the dark.

I swallow. They're all looking at me. Public speaking isn't really my thing.

People always say "begin at the beginning," but what is the beginning? Is it the station loo? Or Uncle John by my bedside? The plane crash? Should I perhaps go further back than that, to Dad's rift with his parents? Or is the real beginning back in a tiny village in Hong Kong?

"I ran away to look for my grandparents," I say, and now that I've started, it's easy enough to go on. It all comes tumbling out, even if it's in rather a muddly order.

Finlay's parents are sitting either side of him on the little sofa. They're goggling. I hope it's not with horror at his undercover activities. I haven't even got up to Zigger's attack on Uncle John yet.

Occasionally someone chips in—mainly Jacqueline, of course. It's an ordeal for her to stay silent for more than a few minutes. When I explain how Finlay met her at the Barras, she says, "Such a clever boy. A real detective." And then I see Finlay's mum wiping away a tear with the back of her hand. Mr. Grant is patting Finlay's knee awkwardly. They're proud of him! That makes it easier to go on.

There are gasps all 'round at the incidents with Uncle John.

"You know he came to our house?" says Jacqueline. "Such a creepy man! I tried to ring you at Mary's, to warn you. But someone told me I'd got the wrong number."

Kenny is looking thoughtful now. "What kind of car does he have?" he asks.

"Kenny—that's pure typical!" Marina chides him. "The lassie's in danger of her life and you just want to know about some motor."

"Sorry, I'm not sure. I'm not into cars. It's quite old. A Ford Escort, I think."

"Blue?"

"Yes, it is, actually."

"Leave off your mind games, Kenny—this isn't the Paul Daniels magic show. Let her get on with the story."

"Carry on," says Kenny. "I just need to find something." He gets up from the fireside rug and leaves the room.

I'm nearly at the end now, but I realize I've left out the part about getting Mary into hospital. I tell them briefly about that.

"Finlay did everything, really," I say. "I was hiding in the wardrobe half the time."

Finlay's mum puts an arm 'round him, and he gives her one of his funny smiles—shy but cheeky at the same time. "I told you I was going to see a mad old lady, didn't I? I do tell the truth sometimes," he says.

"Well done, Leo," says Marina, when I get to the end. Well, not quite the end—just up to my arrival at her house. She takes over from there.

"Finlay knows how I am," she says, addressing his parents. "I'm a bit of a sucker for helping out, and I don't like telling tales. But there has to be a limit. I've seen the mess young Finlay's getting into, and I don't want to make it worse." She grins at him. "That way, I could end up with one of those enimens, couldn't I, Finlay?"

"N of M," Finlay corrects her. His parents smile wryly, but everyone else looks blank. "Notification of Misconduct," he explains in a mumble.

"The main point is that it's against the law to conceal a runaway," Marina continues. "Leo's been reported to the police. She's an official Missing Person. Anyone hiding her is committing a crime."

Jacqueline nods knowingly. "That's just what your horrible uncle said, Leo."

My heart sinks. "So I can't stay?"

"I didn't say that."

"What, then?"

"It's all got to be aboveboard. The Runaway Helpline lot need to know where you are."

Finlay looks betrayed. "Marina! You can't report her."

"I didn't say that either."

"*No one*'s going to grass her up!" Finlay turns his look of outrage to his parents. "You won't, will you?"

Kim speaks gently. "I think Marina means that Leo should make the phone call herself."

"But I can't do that! They'll make me go back there."

"I'm pretty sure they won't. I've been looking into it," says Marina. "The Runaway Helpline is a confidential number. But they will encourage you to see the police and to let them send a message home."

"It's *not* home!"

"Well, to the place you ran from."

"I'm not going to tell them where I am!"

"You won't need to. You just need to let them know you're safe. And if you're going to stay here, someone will probably have to vet me and make sure *I'm* not a child molester."

"But"—it's hard to take all this in—"are you sure I won't have to go back? I mean, they are my relatives."

"But *we're* your relatives too!" says Jacqueline. "You can stay with us, can't she, Mum? I know it's a squash but we could fit an extra bed in with me and Suzanne."

Finlay's mum looks doubtful. "You're not such close relatives as Leo's aunt, though, are you? The way I've been working it out, Kim, Leo must be your first cousin once removed."

"Well, no one's removing her ever again!" says Jacqueline.

"Your grandfather would count as a closer relative," Finlay's mum goes on. She's obviously an expert on family trees. "But from what I understand, he's not keen to own up to the relationship."

"He'll come 'round," Jacqueline says. "We'll work on him, won't we, Mum?"

"You're all missing the point," says Marina. "No one's going to send a wee lassie back to a man who's going to interfere with her."

"Well, he didn't exactly—"

"Come on. What about how he tried to bundle you into that car? When you tell the police about that, he's going to be the one on the run!"

"The guy should be locked up," says Finlay's dad.

I'm still not convinced. "Suppose they believe him and not me?"

"Well, in any case, they won't send you back where you don't want to be. Not if there's a good alternative. That way you'd just run away again, and that would make a lot more bother for everyone concerned."

I'm still not sure. It goes against the grain to disclose my identity when I've been trying to conceal it for so long.

Kenny comes back in. He has a newspaper in his hand. "Did you say your uncle was called John?" he says.

"Yes."

"And what's his surname?"

"Baldwin."

"Read this," says Kenny.

MY LUCKY ESCAPE FROM MOTORWAY MONSTER

EVENING TIMES EXCLUSIVE

A man appeared in court this morning, facing charges of an attempted assault upon a female hitchhiker. The alleged offense occurred at 2 o'clock yesterday afternoon, near exit 12 of the M74.

Lucky to be alive

"I don't like to think about what could have happened to me," said 19-year-old Megan Walker in an exclusive interview with the *Evening Times*. "I just feel so lucky to be alive and unharmed."

Vet student Megan was hitchhiking from Glasgow to her parents' home in Kendal in the Lake District on Tuesday. She accepted a lift from a man driving a blue Ford Escort.

"The man was middle-aged, with thick glasses and a quiet voice. He seemed nice enough at first. When he found out I was a vet student, he started telling me about his pet birds.

"He said he'd been in Glasgow on business, but it hadn't gone very well. Then he started rambling a bit—something about being attacked by a drunk person with a dog or something. I couldn't quite make it out, but he was getting quite worked up."

Lay-by

"He offered me a sandwich, and when I said I didn't want one, he said he knew a country pub where we could get something more substantial. I said I'd rather get straight back, but he turned off the motorway at the next exit. Then he pulled the car into a lay-by and told me to get into the backseat. When I refused, he said, 'Don't you say no to me too. That's one too many.'

"I had to think very fast. I tried to open my door, but it

[Continued on 14A ▶]

[Continued from 13A]

must have been child-locked. Then he got out himself and came 'round to my side. He opened both my door and the back door of the car. He said, 'Don't try any funny business.' He kind of half helped, half pulled me out of the car.

"My mobile phone was in my jeans pocket. I managed to slip my right hand in and punch in 999. I wasn't even sure if I'd hit the right numbers, but a voice answered, asking if I wanted police, fire brigade, or ambulance. I pulled the phone out and just had time to say, 'Help—near exit 12, M74,' before he snatched it from me. I was really scared then, but he must have panicked. He threw the phone into the car, got in himself, and drove off, leaving me by the roadside."

Number Plate

"I was very shaken, but I did manage to memorize the car's registration number. It was quite an easy one, actually, because the letters on it were BUD and he'd been talking about his budgies.

"I walked for about a mile, till I came to a service station, and I called the police again from there.

"I'm definitely not going to hitchhike again. I've learned my lesson."

Later yesterday afternoon, police arrested a man driving a blue Ford Escort with the registration number Megan Walker had quoted.

The man, John Baldwin, aged 46, from Bristol, is to remain in custody pending his trial.

From: Flo Baldwin
Date: 28 October 19:27
To: Runaway Helpline
Subject: Please forward to Leo Watts-Chan

Hi Leo

I hope that you get this email. We haven't had any replies to the ones we sent to your old email address, and I don't know if you've even read them. But the Runaway Helpline man who phoned us said that if we sent one care of them, they'd print it out and do their best to get it to you.

Actually, Mum doesn't know I'm writing this. She wasn't so keen on the emailing idea, just passed on a message, which I expect the man has given you. But there were some things I really wanted to tell you.

It was such a relief to get that phone call and to be told that you're all right, even though we still don't know where you are yet.

I've been dead worried about you. So have Mum and Caitlin. It's been seven weeks now. We didn't know if you were alive, or if you'd got into drugs or prostitution or something. You read so much bad stuff in the papers, but I kept telling myself you've got your head screwed on and that nothing like that would happen.

Also, I've been feeling bad, well, terrible, really, because I know me and Caitlin were pretty mean to you a lot of the time when you were here. I'm so sorry about that. Actually I knew all the time I should be extra nice to you because of your parents dying, but somehow I just couldn't. I think maybe it's because of all that family history, what with our mums not really getting on. (My mum always used to make jokes about your mum being a hippie, but I think she was always a bit jealous of her too, being so musical and everything.) But I don't want to blame Mum because I know I was old enough to think for myself. Anyway, I am sorry, and if you want to come back and live with us, I'm sure it will be different.

The next bit is going to be harder to write. I don't know if you've read in the papers about Dad, how he's been arrested for an attempted assault on a hitchhiker. He's trying to say that the hitchhiker made everything up, and I wish I could believe him, but I think there's forensic evidence, and anyway it fits in with everything else. I need to tell you what's been going on just so you know that he won't be here if you do come back.

Caitlin and I didn't know at the time, but even before you came to live with us, there had been some complaints about Dad. A teacher from the

Convent School near us had reported that he'd been hanging round the school gates at home time, and the police had been round to the house about that. But of course he denied it, just said he was waiting for the bus or something. It got Mum suspicious, though—I've picked up that something similar had happened in the past.

Then, not long after you'd run away, my friend Lily started being funny and not wanting to come round to our house. I kept asking her why, and she just made excuses. But then her mum phoned our mum and told her the real reason. It turns out that one time when Dad had driven her home he'd stopped the car near her house and started telling her how pretty she was and things like that. It was all just talking, but she felt really embarrassed, and when she tried to open the door, she found it was child-locked. He did then unlock it and made some excuse, and Lily wondered if she'd been overreacting, but it still stopped her wanting to come round. Anyway, when her mum phoned, that was the last straw for Mum, coming on top of those other allegations. They had a huge row, and Dad moved out to a flat. He had to hire a van to take all the birds.

Caitlin didn't know about any of the complaints, and she started off blaming Mum for the separation and being on Dad's side. We found out later that she'd even been round there to feed the birds when Dad was away in Glasgow the first time. He told her to keep this a secret from me and Mum, but in the end it all came out. He never said why he went to Glasgow, but I know it must have been to look for you. I don't know how he managed to track you down, and neither does Mum. Of course we've been keen to find you, but he's been acting separately from us, whatever he may have said.

Then another thing happened. He followed one of the Convent School girls home and got reported to the police again. This time Caitlin found out, though at first she still was on Dad's side and thought he was innocent. Dad was going to have to go to court, though he didn't have a date yet. And now this hitchhiker thing has happened. And the worst thing of all is, I can't help worrying that maybe he was like that with you—maybe that was why you ran away.

We heard from the police that a sketchbook was found in his car, and I'm sure it must be yours. So we know he must have found you. I've been trying not to think about that. At least you'll get the sketchbook back eventually. I know it meant a lot to you.

Anyway, I so hope you are really all right. It would be great to know where you are and to see you again. Of course we wouldn't pass on your address to Dad, and anyway he's in custody till his trial. Mum says you'd be welcome to come back and live with us, but that no one is going to force you to do anything against your will if you have somewhere safe to live.

One more thing. We have given the birds to an aviary in a wildlife park. In theory, they're just having a holiday there till we see what the outcome of the trial is, but somehow I think they will end up staying there. If you come back to stay or to visit us, we can go and see them. I know how much you liked them, and I hope you'll be pleased that they have a bit more freedom now.

Please write back!

With love from
Your cousin Flo

LEO TO FLO

25 Dalgowdie Street, Glasgow
29 October

Dear Flo,

I'm really sorry you've been worrying about me.
I should have tried to get a message to you sooner—
but it's been difficult, because of things to do with

your dad. I hope that now we're in touch we can arrange to meet soon.

Thanks for letting me know what's been happening in your family. That must have been hard for you—living through it and then telling me. Actually, none of what you said came as a huge shock because it fits in with my own experience of Uncle John. I can tell you more when I see you. Don't worry. None of it is any worse than the things that have happened already.

The Helpline people have put me in touch with an organization called Aberlour, which helps runaways like me think about their future. I've had a couple of meetings with a nice woman called Shereen who works there, and she suggested that I invite you and Aunt Sarah up here for a meeting in their office.

Aberlour runs a refuge, but I don't need to stay there because I'm lucky enough to have met some very supportive people here in Glasgow. Some are family, and some are friends, though I kind of think of the friends as my family too, as they've all been so good to me.

I'm staying with a couple called Marina and Kenny. Marina has a doughnut stall, and Kenny keeps homing pigeons. Yes—more birds! Yesterday he let me come with him when he was taking some new ones on their first training flight. He put them in a crate, drove them a block away, and then set them free. I was worried they'd get lost or just fly away, but they all found their way back to the pigeon loft.

Marina and Kenny are very kind, but I'm not planning to stay here long. It was really nice of your mum to offer to have me back, but I have a different plan, which is one of the things I'd like to talk about with you and Aunt Sarah. It is to move into a flat with my Chinese cousin Jacqueline. She's living at home at the moment, but it's really overcrowded, and she came up with the idea of looking for somewhere for the two of us to share next term, when I'll be sixteen.

Jacqueline is a student at the Glasgow Art School, and I would love to go there too. But I need the right qualifications. I'm planning to enroll in a college next term to do English and art and maybe some other subjects. And Jacqueline's mum is teaching me Chinese. It's really hard, but I'm determined to learn. It's funny how when Dad was alive I felt completely English, whereas now I definitely feel half Chinese. I think it's because of meeting so many of his relations and hearing their stories.

My grandfather is not so friendly as Jacqueline and her branch of the family, but he does now seem to have accepted that I exist. Jacqueline and I went to visit him yesterday in the elderly center, and I tried to remember the song about the galloping horseman that Dad had told me was his favorite. I sang a little bit of it, and when I got the tune wrong, he corrected me and finished the song off. That felt like a turning point. I'll keep my fingers crossed.

Anyway, Flo, you can see that I feel kind of settled here, though maybe I could come to you in the holidays, if you'd have me. It would be funny not to share with the birds.

Please give my love to your mum and to Caitlin.

With love from

Leo

FINLAY
The Dog Trainer

"Walk quite smartly," said the dog trainer. "Then your dog won't look around and get distracted."

He was talking to the owners of a husky dog, a Jack Russell, a boxer puppy, and another dog, which looked like a mixture of all of those with a dollop of Labrador thrown in.

Finlay sat in the community hall watching the four dogs being walked by their owners around a square made of strips of black matting. This week some mangy-looking tinsel was festooned over the windows.

Every now and then, the dog trainer called out "Halt!" or "Forward!" or "Change direction!" and the owners (but not necessarily the dogs) did their best to follow these instructions.

The Jack Russell, named Perdita, was a newcomer to the dog-training class, and her owner was none other than Ailsa Coutts from Finlay's school. Dogs are often said to resemble their owners, and although in this case there was little physical similarity, Finlay reflected that Perdita was a model of deportment like Ailsa and had lost no time in becoming the teacher's pet. "That's a smashing wee dog you've got there," the dog trainer was saying.

At Finlay's feet, Zigger strained on his lead, eager to join in the fun. "It's all right. It'll be our turn next," Finlay told him unenthusiastically. Going to these dog-training classes had been the condition his parents had insisted on when they agreed to let him keep Zigger. Boy and dog had already attended five sessions without Zigger making any marked progress, and Finlay wasn't particularly looking forward to being scrutinized by the immaculate Ailsa.

Next to him sat Ailsa's mother, a birdlike, breathless woman, who turned to him now and asked him, "Are you looking forward to the holidays?"

"Yes," said Finlay. There was only one day of term left.

"You'll have to bring Zigger 'round to play with Perdie,"

Mrs. Coutts said. "I'm sure Ailsa would like that—she's told me so much about you!"

Just then Ailsa and the Jack Russell were walking along the strip of matting nearest to the chairs and Finlay fancied she had overheard her mother's embarrassing remark, as she colored slightly before moving briskly past. Finlay wondered what she had found to tell Mrs. Coutts about him.

"She said you were brilliant in that show. It was your own song, wasn't it?"

"Oh, that." Finlay had taken part in the end-of-term talent contest. He had originally put himself down to sing "Stone Sacrifice" but had then decided that the song was too heavy for the battered old acoustic guitar he had had since he was a kid. To his own surprise, he had quite quickly written a song called "Running on the Cracks" and had sung that instead. The song was inspired by his adventures with Leo, but the words were too obscure for anyone to interpret them at all coherently.

"Well, Ailsa was dead good too," he replied. It was true. Ailsa had astonished Finlay with the ferocity of her cymbal crashes and the dizzy whir of her drumsticks. It was fascinating to watch her usually settled curls flying about wildly as she threw herself into the performance.

"I hear you might be going to join the band," said Mrs. Coutts, beady-eyed with interest. Did she and her daughter spend all their time talking about him?

"Only if I can get myself an electric guitar," he said gloomily.

Ailsa and Perdita returned, and it was Finlay and Zigger's turn to pace the square, along with a poodle, an Alsatian, and a low fluffy dog, who was being pulled along in a sitting position.

"Lead in the left hand, dog treats in the right hand," said the trainer. "Keep telling them they're really good, they're smashing, they're awful clever, and give them a treat at every corner."

"You're smashing, Zigger, you're really good," said Finlay mechanically. Zigger was as usual tugging at the lead, much more interested in the poodle's bottom than in the treats in Finlay's hand.

"Zigger's so gorgeous," said Ailsa, once Finlay had returned to his seat. Finlay swelled with ownerly pride as she caressed one of the dog's silky ears.

"He's not too bad, as long as no one's wearing a hat," he said.

Mrs. Coutts's eyes grew even beadier. "Have you tried gradual exposure?" she asked.

"No, what's that?"

"It's getting them used to something in stages. You could try putting a hat on the floor, quite a way away from you, then moving it a little closer, and then, when he's used to that, putting it on your knee—gradually moving it nearer and nearer to your head."

"That's a good idea. I'll try it," said Finlay, though he couldn't help feeling pessimistic.

The class continued with attempts to teach the dogs to sit and stay, and to come when called—predictably successful in the case of Perdita and less so with Zigger.

"Don't worry. He's just a strong individual like you, Finlay," said Mrs. Coutts, nudging her daughter. "That's what you said about him, isn't it, Ailsa?"

Ailsa busied herself with Perdita's collar as if she hadn't heard.

The trainer was making his farewell speech. "So, do a wee bit with them every day, and your dog will come on in leaps and bounds," he said. Finlay privately thought that Zigger was all right at the leaps and bounds—it was just everything else that was the problem.

"That's it for the night, then, folks. Have a happy Christmas, but remember, don't let them choke on the turkey bones. I'll see youse back here in January."

"See you tomorrow," said Finlay to Ailsa as they emerged into the mild, damp December air. He wished Mrs. Coutts a merry Christmas and then let Zigger drag him home.

*　　*　　*

"The girls are both here already," said his mother. Finlay couldn't think for a moment who she meant, but then remembered that Leo and Jacqueline were coming around for Leo's final evening before she left for Bristol the next day. Jacqueline had been characteristically mysterious on the phone when they had arranged this pre-Christmas get-together: "I'm like my mum. I like surprises," she had said. "But don't get a present for me because I haven't got you one. I'm going to wait till it's the Chinese New Year."

"Everything's set up in the sitting room," said Mrs. Grant now. She seemed to be in on this surprise, whatever it was. "But I don't know if it would be a good idea to let Zigger in."

It was too late. Leo had opened the door and Zigger raced into the room and was demonstrating one of what the dog trainer called the "bad habits which are much easier to teach than the good ones, believe you me," jumping up and licking the two girls' faces effusively while they did the opposite of what they should have done, petting him instead of looking the other way and pretending they hadn't noticed.

"What's all this?" asked Finlay. A chair had been set up with a kind of checked cape draped over it, and opposite it was an easel.

"I asked Jacqueline to paint your portrait," said Leo.

"And I said Leo should do it, but I lost the battle," said Jacqueline.

Finlay lifted the cape. Underneath it was a curved pipe and a checked cap with a peak.

"It's a deerstalker," said Leo. "You're going to be Sherlock Holmes. It's a Christmas present for Mary."

"She'll just love that!" said Jacqueline, even though she had never met Mary.

Finlay picked up the hat. Immediately, Zigger gave a menacing growl.

"We'd better shut him out," said Leo.

"Unless I try gradual exposure," said Finlay in an expert tone. "That's what Ailsa's mum suggested."

"Ailsa—aha, I knew you were a lady's man the first time I met you," said Jacqueline.

"Don't be daft." Finlay hoped that he hadn't gone pink.

He placed the hat on the floor in the opposite corner of the room, and then returned to the armchair. "Stay, Zigger. Good dog," he said. But Zigger, hearing the sound of a tin-opener in the kitchen, raced out of the room.

"Let's get on with the portrait," said Leo.

"I hope I'm getting a fee for this modeling." Finlay put the cap back on his head and the cape around his shoulders. He pretended to take a puff of the pipe.

"That's great—hold it there!" said Jacqueline behind the easel. She laughed. "Actually, I don't think you look a bit like Sherlock Holmes. He didn't have cute rosy cheeks like you."

Finlay thought it more dignified not to reply, and he was relieved when a frown of concentration replaced Jacqueline's normal teasing expression.

"Don't you think it's a great idea?" said Leo. "I've checked with the ward, and they're going to let Mary hang it in her room."

"I'm not so sure about that. She'll probably decide I'm the long-lost leader or something," said Finlay.

"I don't think so. I went to see her today, and she was much more her old self, giving me all the ward gossip and beating me at pool. She's put on a bit of weight too."

"It must be all the chocolate Hob Nobs the Godfather's been bringing in for her."

"Jim Docherty said she's got a discharge plan. She should be out sometime in January."

"But for how long? Won't it just happen all over again if she refuses to take the pills?"

"Apparently she doesn't have to take them anymore. She's agreed to have a depot injection every month."

"What's that?"

"I think it's more or less the same stuff that's in the pills but injected into the body and then released slowly."

Jacqueline interrupted them. "Could you two stop discussing the wonders of modern science for a few minutes? I'm trying to get Finlay's mouth right. And Finlay, can't you look a bit more sleuthlike?"

"How do I do that?"

"Think about dumplings, maybe."

After a few minutes of obedient silence and dumpling thoughts, Finlay started to feel fidgety and hungry. He was also a little annoyed because Leo was now standing behind the easel and looking as if she was trying not to laugh.

"I think I can stop now," said Jacqueline at last. "I've got the outlines—I can do the rest from memory."

"Let's have a look." Finlay joined them behind the easel.

"No! Wait till it's finished!" Jacqueline laughed and tried to cover up the picture with her little hands.

"I look about ten years old," said Finlay.

"I think it's a really good likeness," said Leo, "even if he looks more like a cherub than a detective."

"I can't help that—Finlay just *does* look like a little angel," said Jacqueline.

"Thanks a lot," said Finlay, who had spent much of the past year cultivating a satanic image.

"Anyway, I bet it'll make Mary's Christmas," said Leo.

"That reminds me," said Finlay. "I've got something for you, Leo." He fumbled under the Christmas tree and handed her the small, inexpertly wrapped packet.

"Thank you! Can I open it now, or do I have to wait till I'm in Bristol?"

"Open it now! I want to see it!" said Jacqueline.

Leo tore off the cheap Barras Father-Christmas paper, and Finlay felt a flutter of anxiety.

"Oh, Finlay, it's lovely!" Leo looked quite overcome as she examined the little old book bound in maroon leather. "*Macbeth,* by William Shakespeare," it said in faded gold letters on the front.

Jacqueline nudged her. "What about Finlay's present?" she said.

Leo put the book down. She hesitated, then spoke slightly nervously: "Finlay, I need to explain something first. Now that I'm back in touch with Aunt Sarah, I've found out about my parents' will. The money has come through, and I wanted to get you something special."

"I know—it's a bag of doughnuts!" said Jacqueline.

Leo was looking a bit embarrassed. "It's a bit more than that," she said. "It's a thank-you present for being a really good detective and a really good friend."

She reached under the sofa.

"Sorry the paper's not very fancy," she said, as she drew out a long, flat box wrapped in plain brown paper embellished with hand-drawn musical notes.

Finlay tried not to gasp, in case he was wrong. But he couldn't be, surely. That size and that shape of box—

"Go on, open it!" said Jacqueline.

Finlay unwrapped the paper. He opened the box.

Inside it lay a black-and-silver electric guitar.

LEO
Glasgow Central

A pigeon strides boldly up to a man with a sandwich, pecks at the crumbs on the white marble floor of the station, then takes off. It flaps slowly past the ticket barrier and away along a platform into the unroofed, unwalled world.

"That one's no' breaking any records," says Kenny.

"There you go again," says Marina. "The lassie's going four hundred miles away, and all you can talk about is pigeons."

I think about the last time I traveled four hundred miles. That was three months ago. I remember looking at myself in the mirror of the station loo. I probably don't look that different now. My hair's a bit longer, and instead of the jumble-sale clothes, I'm wearing the cozy cords and fleece Marina bought for me at the Barras—her Christmas present to me. I don't think Flo and Caitlin will be wild with envy, but I'm hoping they'll keep their mouths shut this time.

"Are you looking forward to seeing your wee cousins?"

"Well, sort of. It depends whether they're reformed characters or not."

"They'd better not be so reformed that you don't come back. Look, it's come up!" Marina points to the departures board.

At first my eyes go to the wrong section, the one headed London Euston. For a second, our sitting room back home flashes before me. Inside the room, a little Christmas tree is competing with all Mum's exotic plants. Dad is turning on the fairy lights and complaining that candles would be much prettier.

But there aren't any trains to the past.

The right train is the two ten to Bristol Temple Meads.

My eyes run briefly down the orange letters on the board: Motherwell, Carlisle, Preston, Birmingham New Street, Cheltenham Spa. The same names in reverse order from three months ago.

"Have you got your ticket?"

"Yes," I tell Marina, and silently I add, "No more fare-dodging, Mum."

This time I've got the right ticket. And there's a return half.